Corbé's Side-Quests For Dolorous The Sketchy Merchant

By
Sir Eli Vladimir

Published by Michael Molina

978-1-387-66899-1

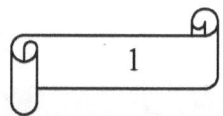

Dedicated to: Israel Molina,

Wealth isn't measured by how much money you have,
but by how much love you have to give.
To the richest person I know

(Happy Father's Day!)

You are cordially invited to:

01110100 01101000 01100101 00100000 01110110 01100001 01101100
01100101 01101110 01110100 01101001 01101110 01100101 00100111
01110011 00100000 01100100 01100001 01111001 00100000 01100010
01100001 01101100 01101100

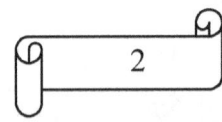

Table of Contents

Prologue: The Secret Cathedral

"This way, Sibyl," I called to my handmaiden, casting my torch behind me to light her way to me.

"Yes, my liege," Sibyl's response echoed through the endless corridors.

Down the passageway emerged the tired, sweaty, adobe skinned, portly, and (indecorously speaking) extremely attractive servant of mine. Gold bands decorated her wrists, forehead, neck, and the ankles of her leather boots. An additional one wrapped around her shapely waist, holding her blue toga in place that only covered half of her chest. Sibyl was braiding her hair at the moment to get it out of her face so to make our continued expedition more bearable for her.

Whenever she was in my presence, I always found myself lingering a stare a bit too long at her. Not at what you'd assume but upon her face. One so pure as if crafted by a master sculptor with big luminous cerulean eyes, perfectly symmetrical plump cheeks that would dimple when she smiled, heavenly white teeth, and a button nose that completed her doll-like appearance. She was more beautiful than any other woman that I'd ever met and I'd seen millions upon millions of delightful women, but none like her.

It was for that reason that I asked her to come along on this journey with me. Although it had taken a month just to get to this point, we had had plenty of delightful times together along the way.

Our relationship had a little snag to it what with her being a handmaiden and me being a king. It was inappropriate for me to develop meaningful relationships with anyone other than another royal. Even though that weighed down my mind, when I looked to her, the whole world melted away.

The melted world, however, rebuilt itself immediately around Sibyl as her proximity to me and the growing confusion on her face retriggered my mind to zone back into reality.

"My liege?" Sibyl asked. "Are you alright?"

"Apologies," I turned away from Sibyl to forge ahead down the underground path. "I just realised how beautiful you are with your hair braided like that."

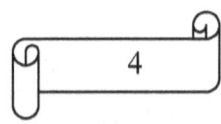

"Ah, well," Sibyl blushed even more so than just from her dehydration. "I've been thinking of wearing it like this more often."

"That'd be nice," I smiled.

"Are you certain this is the proper location?" Sibyl examined the skull riddled cave walls we travelled past.

Usually, those brittle craniums housed rare gemstones for eyes, their teeth would be bared down upon the blades of sideways daggers, and skeleton keys were inserted into their nasal cavities. That was *usually* the case. Right now, it appeared merely like the skulls were just ordinary skulls, their treasures taken. It was a mystery to Sibyl, but not to me. You'd think that after centuries of the caves holding their treasures that dozens of adventurers had come, snagged what they could, and left. That wasn't the case either. What really happened were only *three* adventurers came at different times to take the treasures they thought were most valuable. One took the gems, one took the daggers, and one took the keys, leaving the caves bland and full of nothing but endless columns of morbid stones. Truly, it's a storey for another time, but an interesting one nonetheless.

"I'm positive this is the location," I assured Sibyl. "It looks just like I remember."

It'd been a month of tireless searching for what I'd heard storeys about. It was a location called the Secret Cathedral, a location only known to the Greater Gods and the most royal of families. It was said to be far beneath the crust of Terrace (or Earth, for you unaware). Many people of the Mortal World spread that rumour through legend and word of mouth, but I knew it to be a vastly more magical place than just in bedrock.

The world as far as I knew was divided into different portions at this point in its existence. Terrace was the physical body that tethered all other Realms together, Cosmos was the scientific aspect of it alongside the vastness of space, but I was more interested in Dolorous for my expedition.

Dolorous was the place where all magic existed. The difference between Dolorous and a place like Medis (also a Realm plentiful with magic) was that Dolorous was the place *for* magic. The epicentre and origin location of magic. Its birthplace, if you will. Medis was the place that spawned magical creatures. Although they came from it,

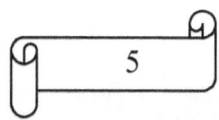

they would make their way to the other Realms to find a place they could call home. It was a thought that passed through my mind as I made sure not to step on any Bijou Weasels. The little rodents were barely visible against the grey brick ground since they were transparent like glass. The algae eating vermin infested the branching, snaking, and crossing catacombs beneath the city of Dolorous.

"Apologies, my liege, for questioning you so frequently," Sibyl said.

"All is forgiven. Your voice is pleasant company," I told Sibyl.

"My uneasiness comes merely from my displeasure of being in this location," She skittishly moved to not allow the weasels to graze her perfectly polished leather shoes that had obtained a few scuffs during our excursion. "This entire Realm is filthily plagued with rodents, is it not?"

"Admittedly, yes."

At a point in my life, I would've disliked being in forgotten catacombs of fallen soldiers and withering relics, but with all the different adventures I'd been going on, I was getting used to it. It became second nature to get my hands roughed up and get personal with my quests. Honestly, it sort of gave me a thrill. A thrill that was absent in my normal life for the longest of times and was welcomed back far too warmly. A thrill I could only find in risking my own life and being with Sibyl. However, it wasn't appropriate for that mindset to be shared with other people of my kind. If Sibyl believed that this entire journey was for me to get my own personal high, it would render the daunting task pointless to her.

"This is important for the progression of our main goal," I assured Sibyl.

"I'd hope so," Sibyl dabbed her forehead with the flounce of her toga. "If I know you like I think I do, then you're hating this as much as I am."

"Indeed," I lied to my handmaiden. "I wouldn't do this if it wasn't absolutely necessary. Watch your step," I warned her of the upcoming ascending stairs. "Don't worry, what we're looking for should be right about... here."

I hoisted up my torch to illuminate a door that was in the exact place I was expecting it to be at the end of the stairs.

"My liege?"

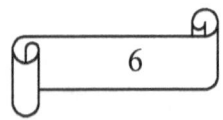

"Hmm?" I glanced over to Sibyl.

"How did you know this would be here?"

"For several reasons," I admitted. "Most of which you don't want to know, but the important reason is that I know this place better than the ones who built it."

In the centre of the doorway was a keyhole that needed to be filled in. I would say that I luckily had the key for the door, but that wasn't true. Luck had nothing to do with it. From my pocket was a hexagonal ruby crest-stone. Imagine the functionality of a key *and* a doorknob in one. Without it, you couldn't even imagine picking the lock. A lot of trouble went down in my history to get the crest-stone and it'd be worthwhile relatively soon.

By twisting the crest-stone, the tumblers within the door all grinded and clicked to allow the wall to be pulled aside. The inrush of air snuffed out the flame on my torch but I didn't need it anymore. Golden light was emanating not from the room but the next one over which was still enough to brighten the area Sibyl and I stepped into. The two of us passed a large ring of statues that I avoided entirely to advance to the golden room whose doors were open ajar.

"The Secret Cathedral is a sacred place and in a quarter of an hour this area needs to be cleared out so that nothing goes awry," I informed Sibyl as I retrieved and slipped on a pair of silver gauntlets from my knapsack.

"What do you mean 'cleared out'?" The handmaiden asked with an air of worry in her voice.

Sibyl's eyes drifted to the space under the door to a shadow that passed left and right in the next room over.

"What is that?" My handmaiden looked back to me as I popped my knuckles and stretched to assure that I was limber. "My liege…"

"Hold this, please," I handed her my bag but not before taking out a belt.

It was a sterling band that was meant to go with the gauntlets. The belt and gauntlets were only three segments of a gaudy suit that I refused to wear fully which was called the Toxophilite Armour. It was too ostentatious for my taste. After a fair bit of weathering on my personality and eroding of my pride, I found that barebones and gritty means weren't so bad. In fact, they made things more personal. They

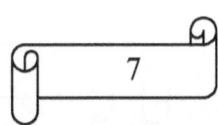

made it feel like I was actually making a difference instead of ordering someone else to do my dirty work.

"Behind those doors is a Lambton Worm," I said. "It's been growing here for years since no one's come down here, so we're here to take care of it before they get down here."

"Take care of it? My liege, with all due respect, you're starting to sound like a... a..."

Sibyl's stalled voice made me pause myself just as I was in the middle of flinging open the cathedral doors. I looked to her, squinting in intrigue and confusion for her to proceed with her sentence.

"A what, Sibyl?"

"A-"

The light vanished immediately in synchronisation with the doors slamming shut against the weight of the Lambton Worm bashing into them.

"We're going to have to put a pin in this for the moment," I told Sibyl. "Stay behind me."

With a few last-minute preparation breaths, I kicked the cathedral doors open, flinging the massive worm back halfway down the gilded church.

Much like the Bijou Weasels, the Lambton Worm was difficult to see but not because it was transparent. Its full gold armoured body beautifully merged into the room's interior, but its hellfire red eyes were the dead giveaway. Those eyes locked onto mine as it clanged its mandibles together and its tongue hissed out of its mouth.

After checking my armour was secure, I leapt into action. The worm bowed its head at me to flaunt its three razor sharp horns, lunging at my torso. At the last possible moment, I strafed in mid-air. As the creature passed over my shoulder, I clenched onto its spiked tail to assure that it wouldn't get close to Sibyl. It chomped its teeth at the handmaiden who stepped behind the door in fear.

"Don't touch her," I growled, bearing my teeth.

With all the strength that I honestly didn't know I had, I flung the monster over my head and back into the Secret Cathedral.

Flicking its tail out front, the worm stabbed its spikes at me which I deflected with my gauntlets. Every move it made was already burned into my mind. It was fast and agile, but highly predictable. Not to the

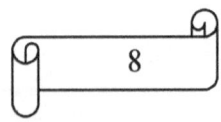

common mind, only to me. It was as if I'd fought this monster hundreds of times. And in that theoretical existence, I would've bested it regardless in every one of our encounters.

Once the beast saw that I was too fast for its attacks, it moved onto a different tactic. After a phlegmy inhale, the Lambton Worm shot out multiple blasts of sludge. In a mundane and annoyed state, I leapt and rolled in between pairs of goo bombs.

There was a specific thing that I needed this monster to do and it was what I needed my armour for in the first place. Only a few ways were known to be able to take down the Lambton Worm, one of which was the method that I was going for.

It seemed like an eternity of the creature thrashing about and doing literally EVERYTHING I *didn't* want it to, but it eventually fell into my trap. With its tail hooking my leg, it swirled itself around me.

"Finally!" I cheered.

"Finally?!" Sibyl blurted in bemusement.

Quickly, I dropped down into the fetal position, allowing the worm to entirely encompass me in its moist embrace. Once I was in the heart of the sphere of worm, the Toxophilite Armour did its job. From the gauntlets and the belt, two-metre-long spikes jutted out in every direction that wouldn't pierce me.

The ravenously agonizing screech echoed throughout the cathedral as the Lambton's innards became its outards. A bodily fluid flood drenched me and submerged the church in inch deep worm goo. As the sections of the Lambton Worm slid apart from each other, I stood up in triumph.

"Woohoo!" I whooped with excitement as I combed the majority of the guts and blood out of my hair. "Did you see that?! I can't believe that worked actually," I laughed, looking at my handiwork.

From my knapsack, I retrieved a small box of blue and red beetles which I released into the room. They instantly began to feast on the chunky leftovers of the Lambton Worm, cleaning the Secret Cathedral to revert it back to its normal pristine appearance. Once they were done, I recollected them into my box and put it back where it belonged.

Although there wasn't a particular conversation to strike up, the cathedral seemed vastly quieter than the universe would've allowed it

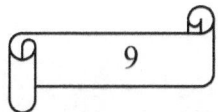

to be. I looked to Sibyl who wore a face more horrified than when she beheld the Lambton Worm.

"Sibyl? Is everything alright?"

I approached my handmaiden, but she took equal amounts of steps backward to maintain our distance.

"Sibyl… What's wrong?"

"What happened to you?" Sibyl said at a whisper which was just like a shout in the acoustic room.

"Nothing's happened to me," I spoke softly.

"You've become one of them," Sibyl's voice trembled.

"Them…" I recoiled in disgust. "You think that *I'm* one of those filthy, degenerate, pretend-to-be gods? You think I'm a *Mediterranean*?"

"No," Sibyl fidgeted with her hair braid as she tried her hardest to not raise her voice. "I know that you are my king. That you are the rightful heir to your throne. That you desire this world to be wonderful and be protected by the threats that are coming… but you are *becoming* like them. Like… a Reaper. Slaying monsters, determining who is fit to live or die, judging the universe in the way that you see fit… All those things you hear me say and tell me that that doesn't sound like a Reaper."

My first instinct was to retaliate. To contradict her immediately. To shoot down the idea that I would EVER become such a thing… That was my initial reaction, but once I gave it a moment of thought…

"You say that as if it's an insult," I coldly spoke.

The response startled Sibyl, urging her to move away from me but an invisible force planted her where she was.

"If eliminating threats and manipulating the world to my will against the tyranny and unfairness of *everything* else in existence makes me a Reaper, then fine…" I flung out my arms, furiously presenting my newly dubbed form. "I *am* a Reaper."

Sibyl's face was that of a sombre sphinx, unchanging, unmoving, and unfeeling. Her body didn't move unlike the thousands of gears grinding away in her head at the implications of my words. Worlds shifted in the galaxy of Sibyl's mind that rearranged themselves and realigned into the new view she had of the universe.

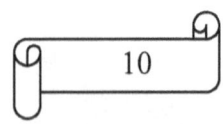

Sibyl turned away from me, whispering softly, "Forgive me, my king… but I see now that you are a force of death… and not the force of nature I chose to so eagerly follow."

I wanted to promise her that I could change, change back to the way I used to be, but she was correct in every word that she spoke. Creepily and eerily, she was correct. Although I wanted many things in this world, being a fool was not amongst them.

"Sibyl…"

Upon approaching my handmaiden and placing my hand on her shoulder, she didn't flinch nor move in retaliation as if she knew that I wouldn't hurt her.

"Before you go, you have to know…"

There were thousands of things I wanted to tell her. Things that could make her give me another chance… but I knew that it was already too late for that sort of miracle to occur.

With a shaky breath, I murmured, "Death… *is* a force of nature."

"Then it will be Death that stops you," Sibyl said as if the words weren't her own. As if they were gifted to her to be spoken at this very moment. "Goodbye, my king."

I allowed Sibyl to slip away from my hand, her warmth still leaving its trace on my fingers. Sibyl stoically sauntered into the passage that took so long for us to find together.

There, alone, I stood at the doorway of the cathedral as I watched my only ray of happiness, hope, and light leave my life. I could've stayed there for centuries, a statue among all the others in the room before me, but time was not on my side that day.

I locked up the cathedral and gave a sigh as I looked at the large double doors that had sealed my fate as well as the fates of the ones before me. Knowing full well that that amber room would lead to nothing but tragedy, conflict, and heartbreak for anyone who passed through those doors, I left it behind with the sound of footsteps approaching.

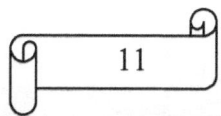

The Sketchy Merchant

Cold eyes stared me down with Hellish fiend-like calculations behind their hazel irises. They burrowed deep into mine, the ones known to burn with scarlet fire from the same sort of Hell. His stoic face was the centrepiece to a vignette of unruly long black hair that was a month too far grown likewise with his beard. We stared down each other for what seemed like what surpassed infinity, but it was me who decided that it had been far too long for the two of us to remain in silence.

"Lancelot," I spoke my adversary's name with a prominent hateful sting. "I'm giving you one last chance. If you're going to do something, do it now."

The two of us held our dagger stares for only a moment longer before he made a risky manoeuvre.

"Bishop to C4," Lancelot proclaimed his move.

"Hmm, not the move I would've chosen," I informed, moving the corresponding piece on the board as Lancelot suggested.

"Isn't that the point of this little match?" Lancelot queried. "To see how differently I think from you?"

"Of course," I half-heartedly said, mentally mapping out my potential victory. "Chess was used by high priests and priestesses to determine the intellect and the militaristic ideals of opposing forces. Everyone knows that."

"It was more along the lines of showing how grandiose and bold one thinks. Chess was designed to be an art-form, not a tournament," Lancelot informed. "It represented three kinds of thinking: Tactical, artistic, and spiritual. All of them played off of the moves that one would make. Queen to E3."

"Is that so?" I raised a brow, taking my turn.

"Trust me, I'm older than the game itself. I didn't make it, but I did know the people who did. A general, a scholar, and a painter all forged the rules of the game in their own forms. The general was the one who sacrificed everything to insure the king was safe, the scholar was the one who finished the game in the least amount of turns, and the artist was the one who toyed with their opponent; playing the game as much as with their opponent's mind."

Hmm, never read that in a library book, I thought.

The implications of the game ravaged my mind as I analysed the board thus far. The majority of the pieces were Lancelot's red ones

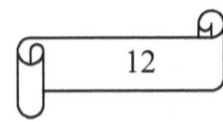

meanwhile the remaining few were my blue ones. Throughout the week, our game had been getting more complicated and long drawn. Lancelot was surprisingly well-versed in the 'art' of chess. Given that the man was the ex-champion Gryphon Jouster of Dolorous, I should've figured he'd be good at all sorts of games, even trivial ones.

With slight hesitation, I shifted my rook to E7 to divert his knight. It would lead it away from both my king and queen, so they'd be safe for the time being.

"All in all, I feel the question you need to ask yourself, Corbé, is: Which one are you? The scholar? The painter? Or…?"

Just by staring at the blue pieces that I'd allowed Lancelot to take in order to save my king, I knew where this was going.

"Honestly, Lancelot, I think the question is: What's your move?" I sternly asked.

A smug half-grin grew upon Lancelot's chapped lips, knowing that his suspicions on my insecurity were correct.

"Knight to E7," He said with me shifting the pieces to make his move.

The reason I was moving Lancelot's pieces for him was that his hands were preoccupied being handcuffed. They were full hand restraints like large thimbles designed to negate the use of one's fingers and palms since those were where most spellcasters formed their magic. Along with his handcuffs, he was in a yellow and black prisoner getup and was behind double layered prison bars. The chess set was obviously in my custody on the opposite side of the bars.

A month ago, Lancelot had killed the king of my home Realm of Dolorous to succeed him. He was thusly imprisoned for his transgressions. Also, for being a total wanker, but that was a tad bit of a personal vendetta on my part.

For the past few days, I'd decided that I would get to know Lancelot better. Not because I was sympathetic over him, but because I was planning for the future. I couldn't keep Lancelot down in the kingdom's dank, dark, and cold dungeon forever. One day I would have to let him free and when that day would come I would be ready. I would know exactly how he thinks, how he strategizes, and in the event that he tries to betray the kingdom again, I'd know exactly how to take him down. My quest on his personality spanned from challenging him to board games, interrogating him on his past, and exchanging storeys.

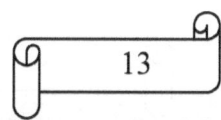

Although I'd never admit it to his face, he was quite the formidable foe and in the event I'd have to face him again, everything would be assured to go my way. No one would get hurt… unlike last time.

I was about to make my move when a chirping noise resounded a bit further down the hall of the dungeon.

"Again?" Lancelot glanced over at my grey knapsack.

"It's probably Black Silver," I rose from my sitting position to retrieve my bag. "I suppose we'll conclude this some other time."

"Ah, yes, Black Silver. How *are* those training regimes going?"

"Delightful. I've been getting stronger every day. Keep that in mind next time you choose to conduct treason on Dolorous," I warned the prisoner over my shoulder.

"The only thing I want to have in mind is that you're taking care of Opal," Lancelot called out into the hall.

"She's being taken care of. At this point, she eats more often than you," I said.

"That's good to hear."

Opal was the name of Lancelot's diamond spitting Gryphon he rode during Jousts. Since he was currently incarcerated, I took it upon myself to take care of her until I saw it fit for Lancelot to be set free.

"Would you shut that thing off already? I'm trying to sleep," Lancelot whined about the chirping alarm.

"It's a long hall, keep your prison trousers on," I wafted away the ex-king's complaint.

From inside of my knapsack, I shifted my deck of self-made trading cards, my sketchbook, and my paint set to retrieve my golden Bluetooth earpiece. It was a little trinket I'd picked up from a defeated Mermaid a month ago that had proven to be an invaluable piece of loot. I inserted the earpiece as I exited the dungeon and assured it was sealed tightly behind me.

"'Ello. Master Silver? That you?" I asked.

"Aye. Where art thou?"

"The usual place," I said.

"Arrive at the Round Garden at your own leisure," Black Silver instructed me.

"Aye, aye, Master Silver," I pocketed my earpiece as I headed up the steps to get topside. "I wonder what today's lesson's going to be."

For a month, every night, a man by the name of Black Silver had been teaching me the ways of becoming a knight. It was five hundred straight days of training and every night was different. Sometimes

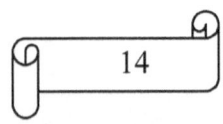

there would be even more than one lesson per day, but rarely. Although a workout every night sounds terrible, learning how to fend off the various threats towards Dolorous was actually pretty enjoyable to me. It also helped to imagine using them on someone I didn't like, Lancelot's an apt example.

Through the corridor and down a few more was the foyer that led out of the castle. The foyer used to be just a simple atrium of grey stone, but I'd altered it just a tad. By that I mean I changed the entire layout of the thing.

In the castle, there was a room called the Hall of Heroes. It was a secret location only known by the people who dwelled in the castle. The Hall had paintings of knights, warriors, and Jousters. Displays contained lances, swords, shields, and armour that used to belong to the people the hall was built for. Likewise, there was a vast collection of Jousters' Caestu in different colours and even more etched designs.

Caestu were items that enabled Riders to mount their Gryphons during a Joust; a leather chord with a gemstone set in its center designed to be wrapped around one's wrist. Without it, the Rider and the Ride would burn up more than likely in a fabulous inferno. I'd never seen it happen, but I could still feel the sting in my leg from when the process started to happen to me.

The new Chamber of Champions (as I liked to call it) was still under renovations and would soon be welcomed to the public. Mainly, security was the thing that needed to be added to the Chamber. After all, it was connected to the palace and it'd have to be watched over so that no one tried to murder me in my sleep. Trust me, treason happened a lot more often than you'd think in Dolorous.

Upon exiting the Chamber of Champions, a particular Caestu snared my attention. Resting in between two handheld mini-Lances was a sapphire Caestu with a feather design. With a melancholy sigh, I kissed my hand and ran it across the display case as I passed it by.

Miss you, I thought, remembering the person that the entire foyer was redesigned for. *All right,* I faced forward to forge ahead with my night. *Let's see what Black Silver has in store for me.*

"Okay, act natural," The man's German voice was loud yet soft, high yet low all at the same time.

His clothes were a mismatched mess of hues. He wore a feathered cap, a loose-fitting tunic, a cape that went down to his waist, and black leather trousers and knee-high boots that were buffed with a

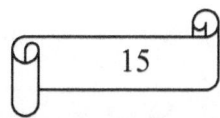

chameleon sheen. The details of his face were a blur, no features stood out. He obviously was a man, had eyes, a nose, a mouth, ears, but outside of that it was difficult to focus on anything in particular.

The stranger within the kingdom of Dolorous walked amongst the busy villagers. Everyone was scrambling to purchase supplies and materials for the big event coming up. Several people bumped into him and stepped on his boots in their haste. He held on tightly to his duffle bag and made sure that it was securely zipped shut so no one would steal its contents.

"You can do this. You can do this," The man told himself repeatedly.

Several stands were being set up in the centre of town that lined the nearby houses. As the stranger approached an area to call his own, he was impeded by a Dolorean rolling their booth into position.

"Sorry, mate," The man shrugged off the stranger so he could go about his business.

"Nein, I'm sorry," The stranger nodded nervously as he backed away.

He tried for another premium location, but another merchant took it before him.

"You new here?" The female merchant asked.

"J-ja," The man sheepishly clutched his duffle bag's strap.

"Then you don't know that this is *my* spot," The woman sassed. "Find your own."

"I-I will, sorry," The man said.

As he continued down the line of reserved spots and pre-setup stands, he found the area for clothing merchants. Despite his attempts, he was pushed further and further down until he was at the very edge of the town square. The lit braziers around town only went so far, placing the stranger in a location shrouded in darkness and unkempt with litter covering the ground around it. He lingered there for a moment, adjusting his nostrils to the putrid smell of rotted food and the not *as* bad sewage.

"I guess this is my spot," The multicoloured man said, sitting at the edge of a sewer grate.

Instead of working on his stand, he took out a pair of knitting needles to complete his work on a magenta beret.

"Hopefully, tomorrow will make this all worth it," The rainbow stranger said.

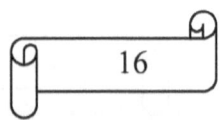

As the non-Dolorean knitted, a single rat with a chipped tooth emerged from the sewer. Although it was initially out at this hour for a nightly snack, it turned its attention to the mysterious man. The rat inched closely to him and stared at the motions of his workmanship. The man glanced to the rat in the middle of his knitting and gave a small smile.

"You can sit with me if you like," The man lightly patted the rat's head.

The rat, as if understanding the strangers' words, climbed up the man's tunic and rested himself on his shoulder.

"Penny for your thoughts?" The man glanced to the vermin on his shoulder which returned a light squeak. "Of course not, you're just a rat."

The little rodent took a moment to sniff the mysterious man's ear before nestling himself right up against his neck.

"I guess any company's good company," He shrugged with his free shoulder.

Together, they sat in their relative silence as the stranger worked throughout the night.

Sweat trailed down my face, limbs, and body as I struggled to keep my breathing at its already hastened pace.

I'd taken the time beforehand to switch into my lesson-gear. It was a grey sleeved compression shirt with thumb holes, black workout leggings, and my normal leather combat boots that were designed for fighting, running, and good looks.

My feet made miniscule taps against the dirt that ringed around the fifty-kilometre circle that was the Round Garden. It was an entire garden that encompassed the Kingdom of Dolorous. It was bright with crystalline fruits and berries that protected the Doloreans with their powerful aura of magic. With strain to focus on my pace, I wiped my bangs out from in front of my face along with my sweat.

Overhead, my beloved pet was gently gliding at my same running speed. Rudy was a teal pterodactyl-like creature splattered with black freckles bearing a pointed crest atop her forehead, a barbed beak, a long-hooked tail, and bright fuchsia irises. She loved to fly any chance she got which was why she always accompanied me to all my lessons.

You're probably wondering why I wasn't riding Rudy instead of running. For my nightly training, it was Black Silver who decided that I would go on a sixteen-kilometre run beforehand. It started off with

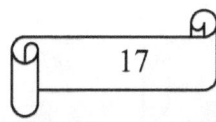

just a half a kilometre, then it doubled, and then again until it reached this point. Black Silver didn't care how long it took me to do the run so long as I got to the location eventually that night. He was the patient sort. However, that didn't stop my determination to get to his lessons sooner and sooner. I'd been getting faster meanwhile Black Silver kept moving our rendezvous location. I was a busy girl and that meant the sooner I could finish his lessons, the more time I could have with other matters. That or maybe it was because I was just eager to learn more of his lessons.

There were some new moves that he'd taught me that made me wish that someone would invade Dolorous soon.

That sounds terrible even in *my head,* I thought, being thankful that no one was able to read my mind.

In the distance, I could see the statuesque and muscly form of my master, Black Silver. The sight of his dark armour, his black panther companion, and his ivory blade injected adrenaline into my system. I finished up my run with a full-on sprint, skidding to a halt in front of Cath and my master. At the distance I stopped, I could make out the rune-like etchings on both Black Silver's chest plate and down his blade.

Black Silver referred to a nearby brazier that was alight with blue fire. In Dolorous, our time was kept by the colour of fire which started red and then transitioned through the rainbow throughout the day.

"Apprentice Corbé," My master smiled beyond his barbute helmet that shadowed his face. "Thou hast hastened thine pace significantly. Bravo."

"Th-thanks," I heaved my chest as I breathed heavily through my nose. "Master... Silver..."

I let out a groan, allowing myself to fall on my bum to take a rest for a tad. Rudy did likewise, landing beside me so she could curl up and have me pet her hide.

"What was my time?" I asked, lying down to stare up at the grey cavern ceiling of Dolorous.

"Only an hour, yet I was not expecting thee so anon," Black Silver joined me on the ground with Cath doing so as well.

"You know me," I tried for my condescending grin, but my mouth was preoccupied with supplying myself with oxygen. "I'm an overachiever."

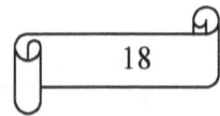

"A fact I most admire, I assure thee. 'Tis a fact that hastens these lessons for thee to become a fine knight one glorious day," He said, stroking Cath's neck.

"By the by, I was wondering, when am I supposed to get a suit of armour? If I'm going to be facing down psychopaths like Count Maleagant or Lancelot, shouldn't I have some armour?" I glanced over at my master.

"Wherefore art thou unsatisfied with thine Jouster's Skins?" Black Silver said.

'Skins' referred to the armour worn by a Rider during a Gryphon Joust. I'd used a personalised set a few times, but that was *during* a Gryphon Joust and it was overly complicated to weasel into. If I was charging into battle, I'd like to be ready then and there, not a half-hour later.

"I was sort of hoping for something a tad flashier," I held my hands up to the sky, imaging my perfect suit of armour. "Light weight, full range of motion, multipurpose, and…"

What colour? My Skins are already blue and white, silver and black is taken, green's more Gawain's pace…

"Dost thou wish to proceed with thine lesson or fantasise?" Black Silver asked me.

"I'm getting up," I rose from the dirt to dust my sweat covered leggings off.

"To understand thine lesson for tonight, thee must demonstrate thine understanding of thine previous," Black Silver drew his ivory blade. "Arm thyself."

A smirk emerged from my face as I aligned my index and middle fingers. A silver aura appeared around my finger-tips. With the energy exuding from me and trailing my movements, I drew a simple cross designed sword and a quartered off three-point shield. The objects solidified to become physical. I placed my forearm in the intersection of the shield to mount it on my arm and clenched my fingers into a fist near the hilt of my sword. Both items levitated only a handful of centimetres away from having tactile contact with me. It made manoeuvres with them a lot easier since I didn't have to physically fumble over myself.

"Run the Dance of Pele," Black Silver ordered me.

I kept my shield close to my torso as I shifted my sword further out in a horizontal position. As I charged for my master, he poised himself to do the counter manoeuvre for the Dance of Pele, Nāmaka's Stance.

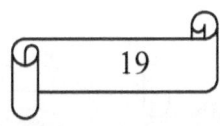

Once I got about three metres away from Black Silver, I leapt from the left, to the right, and then to the left again before bringing my energy sword across to attempt to slam into Black Silver's chest. Motioning my wrist in a figure eight, my sword flailed in the same sort of path. As I conducted the offencive/defensive gesture, I carried out the 'dance'.

Anyone could just walk around a target with a flailing sword, but the point of the Dance of Pele was to not only pay attention to your hand work, but your footwork as well. A hand/eye/foot coordination sort of thing.

As I kept rotating my movements right, left, and further right, Black Silver's manoeuvre was the exact counter to mine. It involved him blocking my sword, going for blows that I would in turn block, and attempts to trip me, hence my change in direction.

The second that I was able to land a hit on Black Silver's shoulder plate, he shouted, "Run the Orbit of Mars."

I leapt backwards and placed my shield on my back. Moving my hand to grip my sword's hilt to give it my full strength. The 'Orbit' part meant that I would swing with all my might over my head to utilise my own momentum.

The Vanity of Venus was this move's counter. Black Silver sheathed his blade to pile his strength into blocking my moves with an energy shield of his own. Using these two techniques against each other usually brought a fight to a stalemate which always called for another technique: Cheating.

As I laid on my arm strength upon Black Silver's shield, I hooked my foot to kick his helmet around his shield.

A chuckle slipped out of Black Silver's mouth as he readjusted his helmet and said, "Run Odin's Judgement."

Instantly, I did a backflip away from Black Silver so I had enough space to pierce my sword into the dirt. By gripping the two outermost points of my shield, I split it in half and sent the two pieces as boomerang-like projectiles. Once they were halfway to my target, Black Silver, I took up my sword and dash-leapt towards him. As if I could glide just above the ground, I wound up to fling my sword like a spear into the centre glyph of my master's chest.

Black Silver poised himself for Loki's Deception, but something caught him off guard. I could only see what happened within the reflection of my master's eyes. The moment before he stumbled

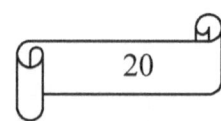

backwards and lost balance, a bright red glint flashed against Black Silver's sterling eyes.

I giggled, slowing my mid-air momentum to firmly plant my feet onto the ground.

"Is that a strong enough understanding for you?" I smirked, holding a hand out to hoist my master back onto his feet.

Black Silver grabbed my hand and with a quick tug, pulled me onto the ground next to him. The two of us laughed with Rudy and Cath shaking their heads in amused embarrassment from their owners.

"Apprentice Corbé," Black Silver placed his hands behind his head, a gesture I mimicked as we lied alongside each other. "Dost thou hath a full understanding of Magic?"

"More or less, but I like hearing you explain stuff even if you talk funny," I shrugged.

"All crafts have their counters. In the heat of battle, one may use a Spell to deflect another's if thee act hastily, akin to combat counter manoeuvres," Black Silver said. "Before a Spell's magic is fully realised there be a moment of hesitation between casting and execution. To halt Destruction, one would counter with Creation. To halt Manipulation, one would counter with Naturalisation. To halt Death-"

"I'd counter with Life," I finished.

This was the sort of knowledge that I wished I knew in advance.

To halt Death... A flood of regret and angst was crashing against the shore of my mind that I would have to ignore in order to carry on with my lesson.

It was a touchy subject that if you are out of the know on, I'll enlighten you about it later.

"S-so, what's today's lesson?"

"'Tis a lesson thee art aware of," Black Silver rose from the dirt and held his hand out in front.

From his palm, six symbols appeared in a hexagon formation. One was a heart that was split into fourths, a skull with swirling eyes, four rhombuses connected to form an 'X', a leaf, a circle in the same fashion as the heart, and an addition symbol with four down-right diagonals coming from the ends and a rhombus in its centre. In order, the symbols represented Life, Death, Destruction, Naturalisation, Creation, and Manipulation.

"Witch-Crafting?" I furrowed a brow. "I know you weren't there to see it, but I think I have Witch-Crafting down."

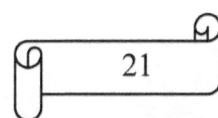

A month ago, I defeated Lancelot in an EPIC Gryphon Joust using some Witch-Crafting and everything I'd learned from Black Silver. Granted, it was a handful of lessons, but it was enough to stop the champion Gryphon Jouster of Dolorous.

"Sir Gawain has told me of thine Joust. Although thine Creation of Fire be commendable, I doth see a predicament. Thee hath only conjured one form of Witch-Crafting. In order to unlock thine full potential thou shall be trained to use all fire Crafts."

"And the Master of Darkness is going to teach me how to use fire?" I pointed out the confusing bit.

"Although I may not use magic such as thee, I may show thee the skills required to conjure such magic. Thee art aware of the passion and drive required for Creation, howe'er hast though conjured any other form of magic?"

"Umm," I pretended to recall, fully knowing the answer was 'No'.

"We shall begin with what thee knowest, howbeit, there be one condition," Black Silver clenched his hands to evaporate all of the symbols around his hand.

"What's the condition?"

"Thou shall keep thine fire burning for a half a fortnight and carryout thine lessons as instructed through this flame," Black Silver said.

"I'm supposed to keep a fire burning for a week?" I asked, poising my hands ready to form my Creation Spell. "Do I kindle it or something?"

"Thou shall place thine flame within the confines of this jar."

Black Silver produced a mason jar from behind his back and unscrewed the lid.

"Does it have an enchantment on it to keep the fire going indefinitely?" I squinted at the jar that looked suspiciously Mortal-World-like.

"'Tis merely a jar," Black Silver shrugged. "Art thou prepared?"

"Prepared enough," I nodded.

With a long inhale, I punched my fists in front of myself uttering a loud, "Hiya!"

Only a few centimetres separated my knuckles and the hovering vermilion discs of light. There were many ways to craft a Spell, but I preferred my method and felt it was the fastest. I circled my hands in an anti-clockwise pattern so they would trail their energy behind. Once the circle was whole, I drew the vertical down the middle and

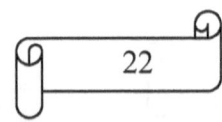

completed it with the horizontal. The finishing touch was to *literally* touch the Spell to activate it.

At this point, I still wasn't used to touching Spells without my crowbar since they'd violently unleash their energy upon contact. I made the tactile moment swift, sliding away from the miniature inferno that burst forth from the Creation symbol.

Black Silver lunged for the flame, scooping it into the mason jar and sealing it up. The second it was closed off, the fire took on a dark indigo shade.

Huh, it must take on the properties of Dolorean fire when it's no longer qualified as a caster's Spell.

"Thine lesson for tonight be over," Black Silver said, handing over the mason jar to me.

"What? Seriously?" I asked, staring at the flame that somehow sustained itself within the vacuum it was no doubt creating for itself.

"'Tis as thou hast said, Creation be a method thee hath experience in," Black Silver nonchalantly spoke.

That's it? Seriously? This called for a sixteen-kilometre run?

"A matter troubles thee, Apprentice Corbé?" Black Silver detected my befuddlement.

"I-it's just…" I glanced between Black Silver and my self-sustaining flame. "I thought there'd be more. I mean, the last few nights you've been teaching me defensive stances, and sword fighting manoeuvres, and battle techniques and… is there anything else for tonight?"

"Ah, aye," Black Silver nodded.

I knew it!

"Something that nigh slipped mine mind," He said. "Thou must name thine flame."

"What?"

"Have a pleasant night, Apprentice Corbé," Black Silver turned away and walked towards the south alongside Cath who meowed goodbye to me. "Fare thee well."

"Fare thee well, Master Silver!" I called after him, waving in my confusion.

All righty then, you mad old son of a bastard sword, I thought, glancing at Rudy who approached me.

"So, I guess I have a flame now," I inspected my little inferno. "What do you think I should name it?" I asked Rudy.

Rudy's gruff growl denoted that she had as much of a clue as I did.

"I'll name it…" I stared deeply into the fire.

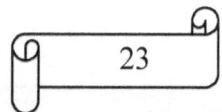

It flickered, it danced, it swirled, and it surged as if it perpetually let out bursts and spurts of energy. No real thoughts passed through my mind except the information my eyes were taking in by spectating the mini flaming tornado. I remained in an audience's silence until I made my decision.

"... Rick."

The Questing Beast let out a quizzical squawk with a raised brow.

"What? If *we* have boy names this thing's getting one too. Not like it has a gender," I justified with Rudy giving a gruff growl. "What? You don't like it? Huh?" I baby talked the Questing Beast. "You don't like it?"

I reached out for Rudy's tail, scratching it vehemently. The Dragon squawked, flapping her wings and chasing her tail ravenously.

"Hey, watch it!" I giggled, ducking under her tail and wings as I cradled my mason jar so to not have it shatter. "Heheh, come on, let's just head home already," I said as I mounted Rudy. "How does a big pile of Tantasteak and some Flaxenrose sound for dinner?"

Rudy nodded eagerly as she waited for me to strap myself in and assure my jar was secure. My little Questing Beast was one of a kind, quite literally. There was only meant to be one Questing Beast at a time so when her mother died, she was hatched out of her egg. In turn, when she would eventually lay *her* egg, it wouldn't hatch until she would pass.

In addition to Rudy being extremely unique, no other creature (Gryphon or otherwise) was quite her size. As a result, I had to cobble together my own saddle for us. The skirt was made from a repurposed leather jacket and the seat was a sculpted piece of ebony that I had a friend carve out for me. Since Rudy was remarkably fast, I found a safety belt and gauntlet fashioned handles to fasten me into place. I placed my jar into my knapsack and nestled myself in.

"All right, I'm ready when you are."

Once she felt I was secure, Rudy launched into the air and veered off towards the far reaches of the kingdom towards my castle.

Black Silver knows what he's doing, but still, I glanced over my shoulder to where I placed my mason jar. *What is he up to?*

Atop the bell tower in Dolorous, right next to the town square, was a panda grooming itself. However, it only appeared to be a panda. When the beast uncurled from nuzzling its nose into its side, its gaping torso was revealed to be a schism that leaked into the infinite universe.

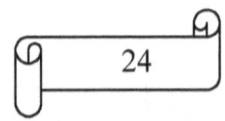

Nebulas and galaxies collided together in the hollow panda's chest and only being bound by a small veil that gave it the illusion of a solid part of his body.

"Ah, Merchant Week, such an abject congregation of hoodwinked degenerates," The panda snickered. "Bound to lament over their abysmal decisions. Not even mentioning what they've *already* paid to me for just this sensational affair."

Mickey Vague was a merchant, much like every other person in Dolorous, but there was something that separated the Doloreans from the panda. Whereas Doloreans worked for Phlorin, the most used currency in the kingdom of Dolorous, Mickey worked for a more universal form of currency. It was known as Tempus. Imagine if everything in every world had a price tag on it and Mickey Vague could see it. He would trade items, turning certain ones into essential stardust or saving others for the next gullible customer that would be enticed by his silk-like voice.

Although the nebulous panda was just a pelt covering trillions of galaxies, that didn't stop his eyes from lighting up at the sight of the wares and his reaped rewards upon entering the tower.

In the bell chamber with him was a smorgasbord of trinkets, gadgets, and doodads that Dolorean after Dolorean traded off to get something they needed for the coming day. They were hard pressed for time and that meant that it opened more opportunity for Mickey to make a deal. It was evident by the room that was so cluttered with tinker toys, pots and pans, building blocks, and old furniture.

"Corbé may have hindered my progress moderately with taking down the Ramparts last month, but ob-la-di ob-la-da," Mickey shrugged.

The panda took one flap of his own pelt into one paw. With a cape drawing motion, the room was eclipsed for a fraction of a second. Within that infinitesimal second, every piece of merchandise was swaddled together into a hiking pack that adorned itself onto Mickey's back.

One item that always hung on the outside of his hiking pack was a forever lit and running hookah. Mickey Vague took up its hose to take a hit. By dipping the hose into his galactic mouth, it conjured up a cosmic storm within the panda's throat. With a broad exhale, a miniscule thunder cloud slipped from his maw. From out of the bell tower's window, the black and grey blur that leaked lightning and rain

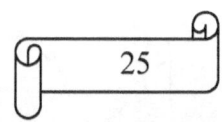

floated high above Dolorous until softly colliding into the Realm's cavernous ceiling.

"And you my friend," Mickey Vague casted his gaze down to the town square, upon the stranger to Dolorous who knitted with a rat on his shoulder. "You have such a song in your future."

From out of his hiking pack, Mickey retrieved a golden flute that he looked over with a solar flare glint in his eye.

"And it's almost time for you to learn how to play it," He cackled.

It'd been a long day of meetings, over-seeing construction, and remodelling the castle that in hindsight I was glad for the short lesson. Sometimes I had a habit of not giving myself a break, so having Black Silver give me one for once was a welcome change.

After dinner with Rudy and a nice long shower to wipe off all my sweat from my run, I swapped into my nightwear which was a blue flannel gown with black furry trousers.

My bedroom was technically the one across the hall, but I decided that I liked Lancelot's a lot better. The one meant for the ruler of Dolorous was sealed off and dark, but Lancelot's had an open stained-glass window so I could get fresh air, light, and see the kingdom at all times. It was one of the best views in Dolorous. Trust me, I'd flown over it upwards of a dozen times, so I have credentials in the matter.

I looked upon the kingdom that was busy in the middle of the night, alight with violet fire. Even though it neared midnight, I knew very well why the Doloreans were up so late. The next few days were going to be dedicated to Merchant Week, an entire week dedicated to selling their wares. That's why so many scents of cooked meats, baking breads, sugary snacks, and sulfur were carried on the Dolorean wind. The sulfur smell came from the recently set off fireworks in anticipation of the event, something that I taught the Doloreans how to make and use.

There would be discounts, sales, and people would be considered for employment. I say 'considered' because most of the businesses in Dolorous were family run and operated, so it was highly unlikely that someone would get hired anywhere outside of their own household.

Tomorrow's going to be interesting to say the least, I let out a butterfly filled breath.

Even though I'd been council leader and eventual queen for a month, I hadn't made what the Doloreans called my 'Grand Entrance'. It was when a ruler would have their bodyguards, court jester, and

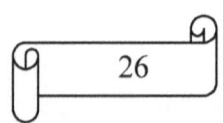

royal adviser, march into town with everyone bowing down. I was nervous for a multitude of reasons. A notable one was that my court jester tried to murder me.

Rudy peaked her head into my line of sight, clearly seeing my distraught demeanour.

"I'm fine, Rudy," I stroked her beak to reassure her.

She was too big to fit in my bedroom, so I had some of my knight-hands construct a sort of birdhouse attachment to the exterior of the castle's tallest spire.

After Rudy pretended to buy that I was okay, she slinked back into her birdhouse to catch a few winks.

"I suppose there's no point in being nervous *and* tired," I mumbled, stepping away from the window to slip under my sheets. "Dolorous, I hope you're ready."

Inside of a palace of purely black metal spikes, octopus-like tendrils, and a set of six humongous bat wings that ended in crookedly clawed hands was the Priestess of Shroudolous, Valaeria.

Dolorous was the Realm that I lived in, but it was divided into sections that housed tremendously different folks. The *Kingdom* of Dolorous is the one you're familiar with, but there were a few others. The Shroud was the proper name for Shroudolous, the sister kingdom where all the Fiends and dark creatures came from or resided.

The tall yet dainty, skinny yet plump, pale yet dark, beautiful woman was sat upon the tongue of the large silver fur covered beast shaped like a throne. Several Shroud-Walkers were entering Valaeria's throne room in an orderly line with fear in their eyes.

Although she was queen of all darkness and ruler of all Fiends, she was still not impervious to mundane tasks as monarch of her land. It was her weekly task to wrangle up all her people and subject them to a census.

With a slight sigh, Valaeria twirled the severed obsidian finger she used as a pen among *her* fingers. The extensive list of Fiends, their families, and their pets was written on the back flesh of a servant. As the list went on, Valaeria peeled the servant's skin like a book page and tattooed the next name. If you're worried about him, don't be, it was layers of yellowish dead meat that took up his back while his front was entirely skeletal. He couldn't feel a thing.

Speaking in a Transylvanian accent, the Priestess said, "Zika and her little Hookworm, Tackle, always a pleasure."

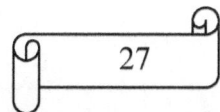

Valaeria gave the purely shadow girl and her pet larva a courtesy smile before they departed on their way. As her 'pen' ran out of ink, she dipped the tip of the obsidian finger into her elegant black velvet dress like an inkwell to resume her writing.

"Zoster," She scribbled the name into her servant's flesh, wafting the vampire in line away. "And lastly Zygomy... Zygomy...?"

The priestess glanced up from the list to see that no other beings had entered her chamber.

"Zygomy?" Valaeria sat up, looking about the room.

"My dear Priestess," The raspy speaking checklist skeleton spoke up. "Zygomy perished yesterday. A mishap with giving their cousin an arm mounted grapple gun."

"Ah," Valaeria said with a combination of remorse and relief. "I've always hated those things."

Valaeria wrote down 'Zygomy – Deceased' and closed the skeleton's back up.

"Now that that's taken care of, time for a bath," Valaeria yawned, rising from her throne beast and tossing the obsidian finger into the creature's maw to eat. "The gremlin saliva is always best at midnight."

"A fact I shall one day test, my dear Priestess," The skeleton assured his queen. "However, your tongue bath might have to wait."

"Why is that?" She asked, donning a headdress of crooked grey branches and gloves with fingers ending in razor-sharp claws. "You know how much I cherish my personal time."

"I'm aware, my dear Priestess, however we feel light on the list this week," The skeleton informed.

"Pardon me?" The Priestess squinted at her servant, approaching him with her newly put on claws at her sides.

"Barring any deaths and permitted visits to other Kingdoms or Realms, we are exactly one Fiend off from a full roster."

"What?!" A burst of dark energy came from the priestess' body as she lunged forward. "Who?!"

The skeleton's flesh crept over his torso to shift to his front so Valaeria could look for herself. She clawed through the pages, her eyes scanning hundreds of names within the flurry of skin and fracturing bones. Her hands moved briskly as she travelled through the entire alphabet. It wasn't until she reached the near end that she stopped.

"My dear Priestess..." The skeleton cautiously spoke. "Who is it?"

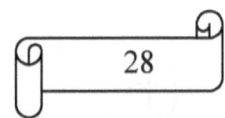

"Aaaiiieee!" Valaeria screeched like a bat getting murdered by a hyper sonic tuning fork.

In a fury of shadows and dark fire, the entire throne room and subsequently the entire castle exploded into bloody piles of gooey intestines and drippy meat. The only things that remained of the entire behemoth of a palace was the skeleton, the throne beast, Valaeria, and a few stray servants of hers.

"Don't archive this until I return!" Valaeria dug her claws into the skeleton's flesh.

"As you wish, my dear Priestess," The skeleton nodded, slightly wincing from the pain that Valaeria was invoking upon him.

"He couldn't have gotten far."

Valaeria unsheathed her fingers and walked off towards the north.

The meaty fragments of the Shroudolian castle, crawled and slithered back together to slowly reform the dark palace.

"Whoever it is," The skeleton glanced over his shoulder to the throne beast. "God save them."

The throne beast nodded in agreement as they watched their Priestess disappear into the distance.

"Corbé," A knock came from outside my bedroom. "Corbé, wake up."

I threw my pillow at the door in a huff. My wakeup call had just interrupted the most wonderful dream. I was in my teens, sipping a fruity beverage, lying on the beach with all my friends surrounding me. The day transitioned into a nighttime camp-out as a fire pit was lit. Just as I was leaning in for a kiss from someone (honestly, sometimes my dreams were a tad hazy), the voice of Raiden Aderyn shattered my dream state.

"Corbé, you know you have to get ready for the first day of Merchant Week, right?"

"Yes, Raiden, I know," I called from my bed, not moving an inch.

"What?" He leaned closer to the door.

"I know!" I barked.

Reluctantly, I left my cosy warmth pocket to step up to my chest of drawers. I opened a drawer and began picking out my outfit for the day.

"Corbé, what's taking you?" Raiden asked.

"Hmm, I wonder," I rifled through my wardrobe. "what colour knickers should I wear today?"

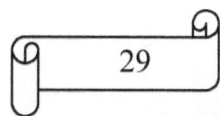

"Okay, never mind. I'll check back in a tad," Raiden's voice trailed off with footsteps heading away from my bedroom.

Finally, I internally sighed.

A month ago, I'd made the Aderyn son a part of my royal council. More specifically, I made him my adviser. However, when I signed him up for it I didn't expect to have every minute of our time together dedicated to him telling me what to do. I enjoyed being with him, don't get me wrong, but that was when he was his easygoing and confident self. 'Royal adviser Raiden' was pretty annoying.

I suppose I just need a bit of questing in my system.

With all the bodily damage, the long days of walking, fighting, and personal losses, you'd think me a fool to say I missed journey taking. Without a Bugaboo trying to devour me, a Dragon trying to slash me in half, or a Mermaid trying to make me join her sorority, my life felt… sort of hollow. Black Silver's lessons seemed meaningless what with the relative peace in the kingdom. Raiden was too serious for my taste considering the circumstances didn't necessarily call for it. Plus, being the chancellor of a royal council was absurdly dull. Lots of paperwork that needed to be done, meetings that needed to be attended, et cetera.

Is it wrong that I want something to go wrong? I asked myself, pulling out my Dolorean makeup palette that used finely crushed minerals and fruits.

I mixed the strawberry with the grey stone to form my skin tone. It took a while to figure that one out by myself. Once done, I added a bit of Kappa Coating which made the mixture one hundred percent hydrophobic for the next twenty-four hours or so.

What do I want today? I raised a brow, staring at my reflection.

I wasn't super into wearing makeup, but there was a reason why I would want to cover my face. Just underneath my left eye was a black birthmark that denoted my royal lineage. It was sort of like a curved 'T' with an 'E' coming out of the first letter's vertical. Although everyone knew I had it, sometimes I liked to cover it up. It made me feel more human (if 'human' was a term I was even allowed to use anymore).

Let's just lighten up today, I finally decided.

I brightened the tone a bit so that the black marking became only a dark beige.

There, I gave myself a grin before freshening up.

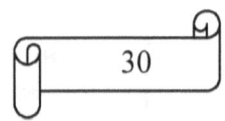

After a quick shower, I dried what little hair I had. Before I came to Dolorous, I took a bolt of lightning to the head. All things considered, having a permanent side-cut hairstyle wasn't *that* bad. The one half of a head of hair I had covered my right eye and went down to chin level.

I stepped into my cupboard to decide which outfit to wear. My hand gravitated towards a black skort, but my hand retracted.

"Right," I tried my best to ignore the article of clothing. "that's for adventuring."

Since I was used to not having that many clothes, I only had a handful of outfits that I wore on rotation. As I chanced a glance over to my first Dolorean outfit, I took out a blue cardigan instead. I put it on over my white vest and slipped into my black skinnies. Around my shoulders, I wrapped a cape that was lined with rainbow plumage. On the interior was a series of safety pins that I added since the cape used to belong to someone much taller than me.

Never thought I'd be dying to wear a skirt.

The only pieces of 'adventure wear' that'd be appropriate for me to wear were my boots and my scarf. I call it a scarf, it really was the previously blood-soaked sash that belonged to Mordred the Dark, then King Arthur, then King Balin, then Lancelot, and now me.

The finishing touch was the necklace I kept close to my heart, an obsidian locket shaped like a hexagon and lined with silver tildes.

Once I was fully prepared, I stepped out into the hall to be greeted by the Aderyn and a group of gold plated knights.

Raiden was a blond haired, blue eyed, teenager who was a foot taller than me. He was in his normal garb of a brown waistcoat, white dress shirt, his rectangular glasses, black trousers, and dress shoes. The only thing that was new was a neck ornament. It was in the style of a bowtie, but instead of a bow it had a coin with a skull design.

"Good morning," The Aderyn smiled to me.

Raiden handed me a cup of hot chocolate, his other being preoccupied by holding a portfolio.

"Morning," I sipped my cocoa with a suppressed yawn. "Everyone here?"

I took a mental roll call of all the gold and bronze knights. The gold knights were meant to be bodyguards whereas bronze were for my musical accompaniment. Before the question arises, yes, it is TOTALLY necessary.

From beyond the cluster of knights which polished their instruments was a court jester in orange and blue. She was a buxom brunette who

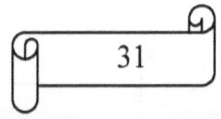

was tucking her recently straightened hair into a fool's bonnet. Underneath both of her eyes were tattoos like single tear drops leaking from the middle of her lower eyelids.

"Tes," I barely made eye contact with the jester.

"Your majesty," Tes curtseyed to me. "I look forward to your official debut as our future ruler. I'm glad I get to play with your royal court," She pulled out an ebony and sterling lute from behind her back.

"Hopefully no one tries to kill me this time," I forced a smile.

There was a reason why I had Tes surrounded by a series of sword wielding knights. Last month, she cooperated with Lancelot to have the previous king killed and throw me in the dungeon. She was also Lancelot's lover, so you'd imagine how awkward having her around was. Despite the fact that she wanted me dead at a point, I felt like giving her a second chance. Well, to an extent.

"So, we have Merchant Week going on until green fire and then we have a council meeting until violet," Raiden read off his portfolio. "Just two things for today."

"Yeah, but two things that are going to take bloody forever," I mumbled, bubbling half of my sentence into my hot chocolate.

"I'll help you through it," Raiden said, handing me a handkerchief.

After wiping off my whipped cream moustache, I handed him my mug.

"Have you lot figured out what song you're going to play?"

"Indeed, your majesty!" A knight spoke up.

One of the bronze knights stepped forward with a long list of songs that the group had written. For as long as the fanfare knights existed, they always did the same song upon the arrival of their ruler. However, I wasn't really into that regal sort of thing. As a result, I just told them to go wild and play whatever their little armoured hearts desired. Apparently, they had a BOAT LOAD of untapped potential.

"Let's see," I skipped over the titles to see the 'in the style of...' lines. "'Salsa', nice. 'Metal', we'll save that for when I charge into battle. I think 'Rock' will go well with Gryphon Jousting. No idea how you lot found out what 'Dubstep' is, but we're not doing that. Other than that, go bonkers."

"All right," The knight giddily rolled up the scroll. "You heard our princess, we're good."

"Here, wear these," Raiden said, retrieving the last pieces for my outfit.

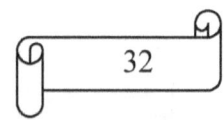

From his brown and black satchel, he produced pairs of arm and shin guards that were dye coated red. The sash and limb braces, just like my birthmark, were signs of royalty. Where was the crown? Haven't a clue. If you find it, send it my way.

With everyone accounted for, the golden knights surrounded me in a hexagon phalanx. As one unit, we marched down the hall with Raiden following behind by a Dragon's length, Tes doing likewise, and the cluster of bronze knights doing the same. A Dragon's length was six metres for those who aren't aware of the Dolorean metric system.

All right, you've got this. It's literally just walking. You don't have to do anything else.

Despite my mental words, I was getting nervous all the same upon walking down the stairs to stroll through the Chamber of Champions.

"Well, Pog," I glanced at the blue feather Caestu in its display case. "wish me luck."

As soon as the drawbridge was lowered and the gates were opened, a dark-skinned man in a white and orange get up hoisted a teal lounge singer microphone to his mouth.

"Ladies and gentlemen," Guy hyped the crowd that clustered around the main street. "Corbé Le Fay!"

With the cheers from the crowd, it was almost impossible to hear the start of the song my bronze knights were playing. Once it came into the focus of my ears, I had to stifle a surprised laugh. It started with a bouncy trumpet beat quickly followed up by the knights beating their armour for added percussion. It was upbeat, fast paced, and in the style of Balkan.

Holy Grail, I subtly bit my lip as we continued our march. *I really want to dance to this.*

With a quick glance at the crowd, the broad smiles, the applause, and the miniscule movements of the Doloreans let me know they wanted to dance to the music too.

You're supposed to be professional, Corbé, I urged myself.

We were about to exit the gates of the castle when I looked over at a woman in the crowd. Her little child was freely dancing, but she settled them down and faced them forward. The grins they used to hold were replaced with faces of stern respect and seriousness upon my approach.

Then again... I let the music pass through me, moving my body to it. *Music like this is meant to be danced to!*

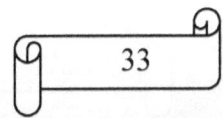

"Come on, I thought Doloreans were supposed to be the fun ones!" I bounced from foot-to-foot as I kept to the pace of the marching guards. "Let's dance!"

Although many of them were afraid to take up my offer, the child who was stopped by her mother immediately took to the music.

"You too," I punched a golden guard in the shoulder. "Like this."

I let my head, shoulders, and hips sway to the fast-paced beat as I let my arms swing in circles over my head. The golden knights remained stoic, however I saw the lead guard's finger twitch on beat.

"Fine, you lot want to protect me?" I burst from their formation and started dancing backwards down the street. "You're just going to have to keep up!"

I picked a random teenage girl from the crowd, spun in circles with her, and twirled her back into the group of Doloreans who'd succumbed to the music. As I hyped the crowd on my way to the town's square, they all began to dance with each other in pairs, in circle groups, or even just by themselves.

Upon glancing over at my royal accompaniment, the gold knights were being snagged off to the side to dance with the villagers. Tes was strumming her lute like a wild woman and Raiden was just shaking his head with a smile while checking his notes.

Him and that planner, I rolled my eyes.

I ran back up the street, took Raiden by the hand, and threw his planner away into God knows what direction.

"Corbé-"

"Shaddup," I lightly ordered, grabbing his second hand.

Hand in hand, I spun the two of us on a prance towards the town square. The Doloreans called it the Quad and it was the epicentre of all business and affairs in the village. It was lined with large houses that were always at minimum two storeys high. In order to save space, every house doubled as some sort of business. There were shops for woodworking, clothing, fresh fruits and vegetables, and a few places I hadn't been to yet. Currently, all of the houses had banners that said, 'Happy Merchant Week', '50% off', or 'Buy two get one free'. The Quad itself was a large square lined with torches that burned with orange light and small river-like pools of water for some of the aquatic residents of Dolorous. Much like the entire village, it was riddled and plated with Rube Goldberg contraptions that ran certain segments of the kingdom. The parts that were most sensitive to noise were reacting, spinning, and grinding as if the town itself was dancing with me.

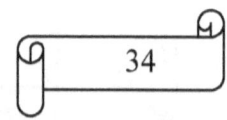

My bronze knights all continued to play their instruments, using the beat of the music to keep up with Raiden and me. We wound up in front of a chimaera fountain in the centre of town when I let go of Raiden. I continued to dance by myself with Raiden awkwardly laughing and standing by. Once the knights concluded their song, I felt it appropriate to strike a pose as fireworks exploded in the air.

Cheers and applause came from the celebrating Doloreans. They threw flower petals of all sorts of shades to bathe the town square and me in a shower of colour.

You like me! Right now, you like me! I giggled to myself.

"Well, that was quite the entrance," A voice like ice, cold yet elegant, came from behind me.

I looked beyond the chimaera statue to discover that a woman I'd only ever heard about was standing in the town square with me. It was the Priestess of Shroudolous herself, Valaeria. I'd heard rumours, folktales, read storeys, and even a pamphlet (written by Raiden, of course) about her. She was basically the queen of all nightmares and was not to be trifled with. Valaeria rarely left her domain so whatever she was here for was not a matter to be taken lightly.

"Then again," Valaeria gave a small grin. "I've heard that you're well renowned for your entrances."

Valaeria approached me, holding one hand up and one hand held outward as if taking an oath upon an invisible Bible.

"I-"

"Corbé," Raiden whispered to me with urgency. "Priestess Valaeria believes in a lot of the old ways, so just do what she's doing."

"Okay," I nodded to my adviser with a quizzical laugh.

"And don't smile," Raiden added.

My grin dropped from my face for a multitude of reasons.

Which reason today? Raiden's being a bossy wanker again? Let's go with that one.

Once Valaeria was close enough, she placed her upward hand against mine. The Priestess overturned her second hand and I did the same. After clasping our hands together, we rotated our positions clockwise. From glancing over my shoulder slightly, I could see Valaeria looking about the village like Sherlock Holmes analysing cryptic evidence.

Handshakes were designed to show that someone means no harm. This one must be to see if the environment was as harmless as the person doing the shake.

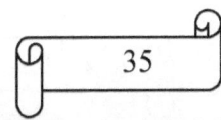

Once we returned to our original starting positions, Valaeria released me from her death-like grip and gave me a full tooth smile.

"I've been meaning to visit you," Valaeria looked me over. "So, this is the new ruler of Dolorous."

"Not yet, you know my contract."

"Ja, I was the first to sign," She said.

"Cheers for that, but with all due respect, why are you here? Not that I mind having you here."

"I have matters to discuss with you, but by all means, initiate your special occasion. I wouldn't wish to intrude on such a lovely festivity."

Valaeria took a few paces backwards, giving a 'go on' motion coupled with a splendiferous bow.

"Right," I faced my public, them staring at me with expectant and gleaming eyes. "What do I say?" I mumbled to Raiden.

"I declare Merchant Week has officially begun," Raiden whispered back.

"I declare Merchant Week has officially begun!" I threw my hands up in celebration.

With a series of cheers, the people of my homeland rushed to manage their shops or begin purchasing items.

"That was easy," I shrugged my cape off my shoulders to hand to Raiden. "So, what did you want to talk about?"

"It is somewhat urgent," Valaeria beckoned to me, walking up to a jewellry stand. "Are you aware of the term 'Fiend'?"

"The blanket term, yes. In the context of Dolorous, no," I admitted.

The two of us inspected golden chains, bejewelled pendants, and sterling bracelets before giving the merchant a warm smile and moving on.

"Fiends are the residents of my homeland. Think of it like my term for a Witch or Warlock for you," Valaeria said.

"Hmm, interesting. Why bring this up?"

I moved us towards a stand that was selling books. Some were ancient, others were in mint condition, but all of them were majority thick and sealed by ribbon locks.

"When I was doing my weekly census, I discovered that one of my Fiends was missing. I have reason to believe that they disappeared off to a neighbouring Kingdom."

"I get the feeling that it's a big deal for a reason," I assumed.

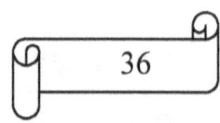

"Indeed. Unlike your kindhearted Doloreans, my Fiends live for causing mischief and disarray. Whether they mean to or not, chaos follows in their wake."

"What does he look like?" I asked.

"I can't describe him," Valaeria shook her head.

"Is that a Fiend code sort of thing or something?"

"Nein, it's simply that, I can't describe him. His physical appearance lives in a quantum state, shifting endlessly in a sort of blur. I wouldn't even recognise him if I saw him and he didn't wish to be recognised, only by his actions may I know who he is, but I'm hoping that you'll be able to spot him for me."

"How's that?" I raised a brow, digging into a thick stack of books.

"I've heard of your very particular set of skills," Valaeria gave me a coy glance.

"Skills acquired over a very long career," I mumbled my reference as I inspected a red leather book's back cover summary.

"You have the Wicked's Eye," Valaeria said.

'The Wicked's Eye' was more commonly known to me as 'I Spy Vision'. In times of random need, my mind would hone in on specific items, people, or events that I needed to pay attention to. Usually, I didn't understand it in the moment, but it always eventually made sense. What Valaeria was implying was that she wanted me to use this as less as a reflex and more of an ability.

"I suppose it can work," I said. "I'll give it a shot."

"And I'll thank you for it," Valaeria bowed her head to me. "I am going to have to tell this to the other rulers so I'll be departing soon, but remain vigilant, my Princess. The future of your kingdom may rely on it."

"I'll do my best," I promised her, immediately getting distracted by a sale item. "O my goodness, Rudy would love this!"

I beamed at the sight of a book that was titled, 'Tactical, Practical, and Fanciful!!! 1001 Aerial Manoeuvres Vol. 2'.

"How much is this?" I looked to the merchant eagerly.

"Today, only fifty Phlorin," The saleswoman smiled.

"Fifty?" I tried to stifle my excitement.

For how useful that book would be for Rudy and me, fifty Phlorin was nothing. I peeked into my pocket to remind myself how much money I had. Thanks to my standing as the chancellor of the kingdom's royal council, I did obtain quite the salary.

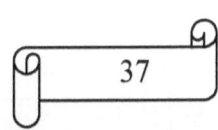

Could do two Tar or ten Ren or just one Aje bill, I nonchalantly calculated, looking at the gold and silver change and my grouping of black, white, and grey bills. There *were* bronze coins, called Wam, but they were the equivalence of a one cent piece and bulged up my skinnies too much. In addition, it just made the looting system vexatious.

I definitely have enough for this, but... I glanced at the merchant table to see the corner of a book that looked similar to the one I was holding under my arm. *Ooh, Vol. 1!* I searched the table with subtlety to discover just under a few spell books... *Vol. 3!*

"How much for the set?" I refocused on the saleswoman in front of me.

"You have a good eye," The woman laughed with a nod.

"I know," I said with Valaeria's voice syncing with mine.

The merchant retrieved the remaining two books from under the piles that she was certainly purposely hiding them under to display them to me.

"All three is just one-hundred-seventy-five Phlorin and it comes with a resizable saddle and a matching set of wind visors for you and your Gryphon. Questing Beast, in your case," The merchant corrected herself as she pulled out said visors.

They were metallic and designed like a knight's helm, but the face plate was tinted like a motorbiker's helmet. As for the saddle, it was beautiful! The base was made of clear crystalline Salamander leather, which could contain and refract light. And the seat was made of Plush Shrub fibers which was the softest natural material in the world.

I do hate having to wear Jousting armour to ride Rudy 'safely'... and not getting bug guts on me would be nice... plus that seat looks SO comfy! But don't let her know you're that interested in it.

Guy, a merchant friend of mine, told me to never seem *that* interested in an item or else they'd skyrocket the price. He also tried to teach me the art of haggling, but I felt like that wasn't really my style.

"Eh, I don't know," I half-shrugged, keeping a cool and nonchalant tone. "That seems a bit pricy."

"Don't worry, my Princess, I can get this one," Valaeria said, reaching into her pocket. "Now, where's my wallet."

I watched Valaeria as she patted her dress to locate her wallet, the fabric splashing like slime and forming eyelid-like openings for her to slip her hands in.

"Ah, here's the little devil," Valaeria perked.

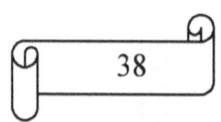

From her nonexistent pocket from her lavish oobleck dress came her little devil. A *literal* little devil. It was a cute living chibi little grey Baphomet that was sleeping curled up in her hand. She crushed the goat demon within her claws, ruby red blood oozing from either side of her palm. The goo solidified to slither and curl around Valaeria's index finger into a much larger and longer claw.

The Priestess pierced the claw into the merchant's table. The blood melted into a small pool which then crystallised into a series of coin sized blood cells, vertebrae, and strips of grey skin.

Gross... but cool! The looting system in Shroudolous must be a tad different...

"Here you are," Valaeria said.

She gathered her currency into her clawed hand and held it out for the merchant. However, when we looked to her she wasn't present. It didn't take too long for us to find her though. By peering around the table, we found the merchant had fainted from spectating Valaeria's magic trick.

"I should really start going to ATMs before visiting other Kingdoms," Valaeria snapped her fingers which caused the merchant's cash register to open so that she could place her money inside and seal it back up. "I visited Frostolous and made a Barbarian jump off a mountainside not too long ago."

"I'd imagine," I said.

While Valaeria took the liberty of placing my books, visors, and saddle into red fabric bags for me, I placed the 'Closed' sign on the front of the merchant's table.

"Pleasure doing business," I said as Valaeria and I scooted away from the unconscious merchant. "Thank you, Valaeria," I smiled to my sister in sovereignship.

"You are most very welcome. I'm going to take a gander at the other booths around here, but I shall be on my way soon. I need some winter gear if I'm going to be passing through Frostolous and informing the other rulers."

"All right, tell them I said 'ello."

"I will, fare well for now, Princess Corbé."

"Fare well for now, Priestess Valaeria!"

I waved her goodbye before turning my attention to the business filled Quad.

"What did Valaeria want to talk to you about?" Raiden walked up to me, dusting off his planner that he apparently located.

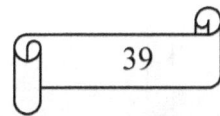

"Just a Fiend that may or may not be in Dolorous. Don't worry, we've got some shopping to do."

All my life, I'd been going off of scraps, salvaged clothes, and hand-me-downs. Could you blame me for wanting to spoil myself for once? If you can, shaddup.

I handed Raiden my bags so that my hands were free to shop.

There are *some perks to having Raiden follow me around all day after all.*

"Seriously?" Raiden asked blankly.

"Yes, seriously. Come along, I'll buy you a new eyeglass frame or something."

I wafted Raiden over to a nearby stand that sold eyewear of all sorts.

"Corbé!" A high-pitched cheer came from off to the side.

A heavily-muscled apron-wearing Eagle creature eagerly stepped up to me. More specifically, he was known as a Burrowing Eagle (or a Grinoff if you want to be P.C.). They were a subspecies of Gryphons that evolved to not have wings. Instead, they developed their arm muscles so they could dig. In addition, they had sunglass lenses for eyes, torches fixed into their foreheads, bronze quills on the majority of their bodies, orange and green for their tailfeathers, and they always wore hats. This one in particular wore a red and white snapback cap with a green hexagon on its front. It was his hat that gave him his nickname.

"Snapback!" I greeted the Burrowing Eagle and patted my fist against his lightly. "How have you been?"

"I've been better, but it doesn't matter. I have something for you!" Snapback reached into his apron. "I heard that Merchant Week was happening so I decided to make these!"

Snapback held out a group of twine cords with names that I recognised on them made out of scrap metal.

Corbé, Cath, Sir Paul, Gawain... Wait...

"Aww, Snapback. Are these friendship bracelets?"

I wasn't really into the whole girly scene, but apparently Snapback was which sent a warm tingle into my heart.

These are so cute, I thought, picking up the bracelet with my name on it. *They're cheap, they're frail, they look like they were pulled out of a garbage disposal, and they're perfect!*

"If this is for Merchant Week, how much is it?" I asked.

"What do you mean?" Snapback tilted his head. "You just ask a merchant for what you want and they give it to you, right?"

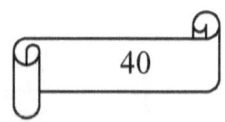

"Psst, Corbé," Raiden whispered to me, turning his friendship bracelet over in his hand. "Snapback's lived in the Utmost Underground for his entire life. I don't think they have an economic system down there."

"Right," I faced back to the little Grinoff. "Snapback, merchants 'sell' people things, which means that they get something back in return when they give someone their wares."

"Ah…" Snapback scratched his chin, wondering what he could possibly want before flinging his arms wide with a broad grin. "Hugs?"

"Fair enough," I gave Snapback an embrace to finalise our transaction.

I fastened the friendship bracelet around my wrist as Snapback tackled Raiden with a hug.

"Oof," Raiden strained to carry my bags *and* the half-tonne Grinoff. "I think I'm overpaying."

"D'aww, Raiden, you're so generous," I giggled, trying on a pair of green tinted sunnies for size.

Among the chaos that was the Quad, there was one merchant's stand that was relatively untouched. It was a tailor's stand who was selling multicoloured clothes, accessories, and bags. The merchant was sat in the far corner of the Quad, wrapping a length of yarn around a small doll. With a miniscule breath upon the doll, the rainbow of colour shifted to become majority white with the dozens of shades becoming smaller. As the multicoloured garbed merchant placed his newest doll into a wicker basket of dozens more, a woman approached his stand.

"Hallo, ma'am. What brings you by?" The man spoke in his perplexing way of speech.

The woman looked through the merchandise before finding a thick winter sweater.

"How much is this?" The woman asked the rainbow-coloured merchant.

"It took me a month to knit that myself and it's guaranteed to hold together for over a lifetime. I'd say about fifty Phlorin," The merchant set the price.

"Fifty Phlorin?" The woman asked in disgust. "Why so high?"

"Like I said," The merchant slightly retracted with a lighter tone. "It took a long time to make and… it will last forever. It contours to one's body upon growth."

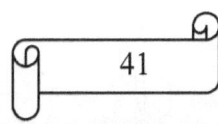

"Well, I'm not hitting a growth spurt and I'm not planning on gaining any weight," She roughly placed the sweater back onto the table.

The merchant delicately hovered his hands over the sweater as if to see if it was okay.

"I-I guess twenty-five Phlorin would work," The merchant rubbed the back of his neck.

"I suppose, but what is with the colour? No one's going to want to be seen in this, least of all me."

"That's easily changeable. I can just-"

"I wonder what Tes has at *her* stand," The woman walked towards the court jester's booth before the rainbow merchant called to her.

"Ten Phlorin?" The merchant offered.

"More like five," The woman said.

The rainbow merchant sadly stared at his creation before handing it to the woman.

"Deal," He said.

With the transaction of a single silver Ren, the woman walked off with the sweater without a single word. From below the booth, the merchant's new rat friend came up onto the table. He tilted his head at the merchant who sadly patted the vermin. The merchant huffed out a sigh, sitting down on his chair and looking at the one piece of Phlorin he had to show for his hard work for the entire day.

After a long day of shopping, speaking with the commoners, and a nap, I was totally prepared for Black Silver's lesson. Yesterday was a different storey. I already knew how to channel Creation powers, but today I was excited to learn how a new method of Witch-Crafting was done.

Overhead during my run to Black Silver's lesson area, Rudy was rolling through the sky in a cannonball fashion while wearing her new wind visor and saddle. Every few metres, she'd whip out her wings, give herself a boost, and roll back up into a ball. That manoeuvre was called the Cannon Roll. It was a method to fly faster with less effort, but it was a move that was advised to only be done by the flier and not with a Rider. And yes, that was one of the moves from my new books.

Money well spent, I smiled at Rudy over my shoulder who was having the time of her life.

In the centre of a dirt patch surrounded by six tall wooden posts was my master. Black Silver was reclined against Cath's tum, scraping his

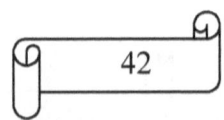

finger against the edge of a rounded blade. The contact sharpened the piece of metal with light sparks being shaved off.

Upon arriving at the rendezvous spot, I nearly tripped but managed to salvage my entrance. I threw myself into it, flipping forward, and sticking the landing in a 'Y' stance.

Praise the sun, wenches.

"'Ellooo, Master Silver," I sang.

"Apprentice Corbé," Black Silver rose from his relaxed position. "Yet another record time, shall I move our rendezvous locations vastly further?"

"You know I'm game," I gave a cocky grin to my master.

"Hast thou brought thine flame?" Black Silver asked.

"Yes, sir."

I whistled so that Rudy would land right next to me. From her saddle pouch, I retrieved my mason jar.

Outside of Creation, I'd never really seen what other methods of magic could do, so this was the first form of excitement I had in almost a month.

"Thine next lesson 'tis of Naturalisation," Black Silver informed me.

"Naturalisation," I repeated in wonderment for emphasis. "What does that do?"

"'Tis a method of Witch-Crafting to let loose the powers of any magic chosen. Roots shall grow with haste, water shall crash disastrously, and in thine case fire shall spread wildly. Naturalisation be a sensitive practise. 'Tis not in thine full control, only in thine suggestion. The element shall always run its course, howbeit it shall listen to its Crafter's suggestions if they be powerful enough."

"So, it's like babysitting a flame? Letting it have fun, but not too much fun?" I asked.

"Verily," Black Silver lightly chuckled in his throat. "I hath selected our area carefully. Thee shall let loose thine flame and let it spread but not burn down these six pillars."

"I was wondering what those were all about," I glanced around at our environment again.

"Set thine flame upon the kindling and await instruction," Black Silver told me.

"Aye, aye."

I undid the lid and tilted the mason jar into the firepit at the six-pillars' centre. The flame tumbled out of the jar like a burning tennis ball and instantly took to the kindling. I backed away from it as the fire

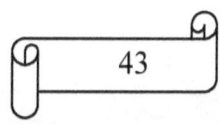

became two metres high. The sight of a fire that was bigger than me slightly left me unnerved since I had plenty of experiences with things of that sort. By the by, none of them were overly fond memories.

"Form thine Spell as such," Black Silver said.

Black Silver started off with the cross that was in the centre of all Spells. He drew an 'X' that was half the size of the cross and shared its centre. Lastly, he drew a border around it that made it look like a smooth-edged leaf. Without a target to lock onto, the Spell disappeared into black dust.

"Thou must acknowledge that somethings may be out of thine control. Thine flame may be of thine own creation, howe'er 'tis not thine when set free. Naturalisation be not control of thine Spell, merely the cautious and worried warnings of a perceived parental being."

"You're acting like I'm supposed to be the mother of a flame," I laughed with Black Silver not doing likewise. His silence left my laughter trailing off into awkward giggles.

Ooookie dokie then...

I mimicked the motions of Black Silver to produce a red leaf in front of myself. Black Silver and Cath backed away from the bonfire in a way that made me less confident in how this was going to go. Once they were out of the ring of wooden pillars, I decided to start up the Spell.

All right, Corbé. Let's try this out. No different than any other Spell.

Unlike the Creation Spells I was used to, the Spell drifted to the only thing it could work with which was my flame. It disintegrated against the fire and almost immediately spread it two metres further from the pit. I stumbled back to make sure that the flames wouldn't singe me.

"Steel thine nerves, show no fear. Although the Spell is no longer thine, 'tis still a part of thee. Tell the flame what to do and await to see if it listens," Black Silver raised his voice to supersede the crackling growls of the growing inferno.

You trained Rudy how to fly, how hard can this be? I glanced over at the dragon overhead who was hovering in a circular holding pattern, being vigilant on standby just in case she needed to swoop in. *Corbé, what the heck are you talking about? Teaching a Dragon to fly and a fire to NOT burn are two drastically different things! Focus.*

"Concentrate on thine Spell despite its destruction," Black Silver advised, seeing my insecurity over taming the flame.

With a stilling breath, I focused my mind's eye on the red Spell-Casting symbol I created. As if electricity was travelling through my

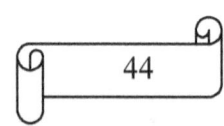

forearms, my invisible Spell tensed my nerves. The unseen energy curled my fingers and locked my knuckles. The inferno surpassed the wooden posts and was now spreading even further. I could feel the power of the fire in my body, crippling me like it was gradually going to do to the wooden posts.

"Concentrate," Black Silver repeated. "Inform thine flame of where it must reside."

Even though the fire was becoming monumental in front of us, Black Silver and Cath seemed to be pretty level-headed.

As the mental image of my Spell became clearer and I burrowed my vision into the fire, I honed my mind to focus on nothing but the flame. When a tendril of fire would flick out of the base, my eyes darted in a sort of lightly scolding fashion. The blue flame was spreading across the dirt to the grass of the Withered Woods, but I moved my hand towards it as if to say, 'Halt!'. The flame hit an invisible wall, recoiling backwards behind the burning posts. I repeated the action on the opposite side so that it wouldn't singe Cath's whiskers. When the fire tried to move past my imaginary boundary, I conducted a swiping motion which immediately made a portion of the fire retreat.

Hold on a tic… Is it really that simple?

I glanced over at Black Silver who was just staring at my flame's progress.

Can't hurt to try.

In an experimental procedure, I rotated one hand to realise that the fire was specifically listening to my directions. Although it seemed like it was an impossible angle, it avoided an invisible bubble of air. It was like I was a glass blower that was morphing an impending crystalline masterpiece.

A grin grew upon my face once I saw exactly how this worked. I made wave motions around the inferno, smoothing its edges. Swirling my hands in circles caused it to spiral in a column that compressed its circumference. Soon enough, the fire was burning high, but no further than the charred wooden posts that still stood tall.

"Bravo, mine apprentice," Black Silver gently clapped his metallic palms together. "Thou hast done well."

"I'd say so, yeah," I said, dabbing my hairline of the sweat that had formed from my mental workout.

"Now then…"

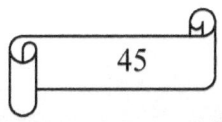

Black Silver took up my mason jar and threw it into the indigo inferno. The fire was sucked into the tiny piece of glassware and allowed my master to seal it up.

"Thou art done for thine lesson," Black Silver held the mason jar out for me.

"Master Silver?" I asked, taking the jar from him.

"Yes, Apprentice Corbé?"

"Why are my lessons so short lately?"

"Lay thine trust upon me, Apprentice Corbé, thine lessons serve a purpose. For now, enjoy thine time to thyself," Black Silver gave me a nod before heading back where he walked off last night.

They might serve a purpose, I just wish I knew what it was.

"Come on, Rudy. Come on, Rick," I said, retrieving my wind visor helmet and mounting myself and Rick onto Rudy's back. "Let's get some rest."

Beyond a rose gold mountain and a swamp thick with sludge and fog resided a fragmented series of floating clay blocks, charcoal, tree branches covered in marigolds, and inextinguishable technicolour fire. The levitating litter churned in the air like a slowly forming tornado.

Approaching from the south was the Fiend Queen with several shopping bags across her forearms adorned in a thick black furred coat and a large pair of mountain sunglasses. Valaeria hummed to herself, shoving her claws into her gelatinous pocket. Upon removing her hand from her dress, a crystal bracelet was wrapped around her wrist.

Valaeria hefted her hand up to the cluster of random earth shards. The rainbow fire fragments darted for the priestess' wrist, getting sucked into her bracelet. For a moment, an aurora surged through the bracelet before being shot back at the assortment of hovering rubbish. Upon their collision and subsequent fantastical explosion, the earthen shrapnel compressed together into a massive ring that opened a window that displayed an icy tundra so thick with snow that the lights of a far-off settlement were barely visible.

As the Priestess pocketed her bracelet and was about to head into the portal, she heard a sly and smooth voice behind her.

"That Neither Ring... Be careful with it. I know plenty of people that would *love* to have it," Mickey Vague chuckled.

Valaeria glanced off to the side to find the hookah sucking panda sitting on a tree stump. The two of them stared at each other with both of their eyes not registering any emotion.

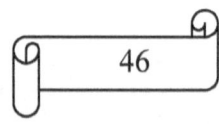

"I heard about your situation," Mickey sipped his hose. "I'll be sure to do my part. Just call it my good deed for the week."

Although the features on Valaeria's face didn't move a single Planck length unit, it was obvious she wanted to say something to the conniving throw rug. The only thing that the Priestess could muster was a single nod to the panda before stepping through the portal. Once the sovereign was gone, the gateway exploded back into its base components to be added into the atmosphere once more.

"Heheheh," Mickey packed up his hookah and got on all fours to head to the kingdom again. "I think it's almost time to pay the Piper a little visit."

Another day, another morning routine. Luckily, since I'd already done my grand entrance, it would carry throughout Merchant Week. I didn't know why, but I was super tired when I woke up. I got cleaned up and dressed with slight discomfort.

I slipped on a green cardigan and a loose fitting black vest just fine, but it was squeezing into my skinnies that was the problem.

"The heck?"

I tugged on the belt loops of my trousers to try to slip them over my thighs.

"Come on, I know I ate a few Flaxenrose in town, but not *this* many," I griped.

"Corbé," Raiden knocked on my door. "Are you all right in there?"

"Give me a tic!" I hollered.

With light grunts, I was able to slip my trousers on, but now there was a different challenge.

The button...

I grabbed both sides of my trousers and strained to bring the two halves together. In my attempt to button my fly, I fell back on the ground and was now thrusting violently to try to aid the process.

Did these shrink or something? They... fit... yester... day!

"We're going to be late," Raiden said.

"I know!" I barked at Raiden.

Bugger this.

I aborted the mission to retrieve my workout leggings in replacement. After a few sprits of perfume, they were 'suitable' to wear in town. I tied my scarf and clipped my cape around my neck and rushed out the door.

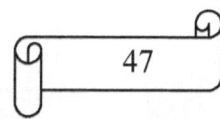

"Morning... Corbé..." My royal adviser spoke in a distraught nature.

Raiden stared at me strangely. More specifically, he stared at the top of my head.

"Hey," I said, massaging my waistline where I now had light fabric burns. "What's up? What's wrong? Do I have something in my hair?"

"No, it's just..." Raiden placed a hand on his head and drew an imaginary line to mine. "Did you get taller?"

"What?"

When I woke up, I must've not realised that things seemed... different. My cape was now drawn up to the middle area of my shins. In addition, Raiden didn't have to look down a foot to make eye contact. Judging from our current height differences, I'd grown six inches over the course of one night.

That explains my trousers. Great, I just got outfits that fit me. Why'd I have to have a growth spurt now*?*

"Let's just head to town all ready, I need to buy some new clothes," I said, checking how much Phlorin I had on me.

"Uh, Corbé. I think we should probab-"

"Raiden," I abruptly faced him, halting him in his tracks. "I don't know why, but today isn't the day to annoy me with one of your patented 'Raiden monologues'. Okay?"

I continued on my way to the foyer with Raiden still standing in the hall outside my bedroom. The Aderyn son squeezed his planner in his gob-smacked state. Once he was able to shake himself out of his shock, he adjusted his neckpiece and trailed behind me.

"Okay..."

In town, I headed directly for the grouping of booths that were most plentiful in articles of clothing. Although Tes was the most well-known tailor in the kingdom, there were a few smaller merchants trying to sell their own apparel. The downside of Tes being the tailor since the dawn of time was that everyone only knew how to make clothes in her sort of style.

As Raiden and I passed the various booths of copy-cat shirts and familiar looking trousers, an accidental yawn slipped out from my mouth.

"Is this really everything they've got here?" I asked, glancing over a rack of cardigans that looked just like the one that I currently wore.

"Were you hoping for something more unique?" Raiden asked.

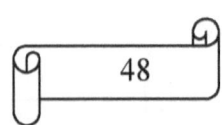

"Yeah," I kept my voice low so that the merchants wouldn't hear me. "I mean, everything looks the same and they're all for the same price. I don't really see the point in buying any of these."

"Maybe you should just get Tes to get your clothes altered," Raiden offered.

"I guess," I sighed, fanning myself with my bills. "I was sort of hoping to get something new today."

Just as we were about to turn around to head back towards Tes' booth, a multicoloured wall of cloth caught my eye. Since it was in the clothing area of the Quad, I was compelled to infer that it was indeed a merchant selling peculiar clothing.

"Hold on a tic, let's see what this one's got," I said, leading Raiden towards the last booth in the Quad.

The closer I got to the booth, the more articles I could see. Each glove, sock, trouser, vest, blazer, and even bag was made up of yarn that was braided with a rainbow of hues. I'd imagine many people would find it odd, but to me it was sort of like the friendship bracelet that I got from Snapback. The clothes were odd in a cute sort of way.

Tacky! Tacky is the word. I love tacky, I mentally perked as I instantly fell in love with a pair of mittens that could fold into fingerless gloves. *This would be nice for whenever I want to visit Frostolous.*

From a small backroom came an obscure man eating a bowl of corned beef hash with a rat on his shoulder munching on a carrot. The sight of me looking at his merchandise caused both of them to choke on their food.

As I looked up from the booth, all of space/time slowed down. My eyes darted from item to item before zooming in on the man in front of me. His clothes were all shades of Dolorean fire, his stature was tall but sort of creepily slouched, and his face was indescribable.

This has got to be the one Valaeria talked about, I told myself. *Keep calm. Don't scare him. Wouldn't want him to stir up any of Valaeria's supposed 'mischief'.*

"Ms...." The merchant coughed as he placed his food down so he could address me properly. "Ms. Le Fay," He bowed to me.

"Just call me Corbé," I smiled to the merchant, fiddling with the mittens in my hands.

"W-what brings you by?" The merchant asked, slipping an Ever Chill (a mint pastry) into his mouth to freshen his breath as he dusted his clothes off.

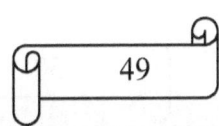

"Well, it's Merchant Week and you're a merchant, right?" I lightly teased the salesman.

"J-ja, I-I am. I am a merchant," He said, his stature straightening. "I just didn't think that you of all people would want anything from me. You're well known for your flair and style."

"I-"

"Corbé loves tacky stuff," Raiden informed the merchant, flipping through his portfolio.

"I think these are all so cute," I passed my hand over all of the accessories laid out on the table delicately like I was petting a newborn kitten.

"Really?" The merchant genuinely asked.

"Is there anything else you have?" I asked, glancing over the merchant's shoulder to see his backroom filled with other wares.

"Ja," The merchant said. "If you want, you can look for yourself. I have the rest in the changing room."

"Perfect," I grinned, handing the mittens to Raiden. "Make sure no one takes these."

I made my way to the backroom and shut the door. There were heavy coats, scarves, neckerchiefs, skorts, dresses, and hats.

I hate *dresses, but...* I eyed the one-shoulder dress hanging in the corner of the changing room. *What is up with me today?*

In a sort of snap decision, I stripped down and slipped into the dress. After checking to see if I put it on right, I stepped out to get a second opinion.

"Oi, Raiden," I said. "What do you think?"

Raiden glanced up from his papers and had to double take to confirm the odd sight of me in a dress. For the first time since I made him my adviser, Raiden voluntarily lowered his portfolio from his face to give me his undivided attention.

Hmm, maybe dresses aren't that bad, I smiled at the success of my own personal goal. *Get Raiden to look away from his timetable: Check.*

"Well?" I did a twirl to show off both sides of the dress.

"I-I th-think..." Raiden gulped. "You're..."

The stare Raiden held upon me was with a gentle sort of dream state, but he caught himself which brought him to a bright red blush.

"Your colour's more black, isn't it?" Raiden said.

Raiden... I mentally sighed, my shoulders drooping slightly.

"I can fix that! I can fix that," The merchant hastily jumped in.

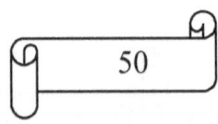

"Is there a black one in there?" I asked, glancing at the dressing room and wondering if I'd missed something.

"Nein," The merchant shook his head. "*This* is the black one."

A white translucent breath left the merchant's mouth to be piled into his palm in a ghost-like snowball. He ran a hand through it which sent the air into several tendrils around me. The white tentacles slipped into the seams of the dress and altered the pigments to turn it completely black.

"Whoa," Raiden adjusted his glasses to see if he saw what just happened properly.

"How'd you do that?" I asked in wonderment, inspecting the dress.

Although the dress seemed to be black, upon a vastly closer inspection, it was every colour clustered tightly together.

"It's just something that I was born with," The merchant said. "If there's anything you want the colour of changed, I can change it."

"To what extent?" I asked.

The merchant let out a long-drawn breath which changed up the dress even further. Not only could he alter the colour, but the pattern on it too. Dragons, zig-zags, flowers, and flames all appeared and were replaced with each other in quick succession like I was wearing a fashion forward kaleidoscope.

"That's awesome!" I shouted in shock and awe.

Not only did this booth have so many unique pieces of clothing, but they could literally look like anything!

If this is the Fiend that Valaeria warned me about, I wonder if she'll let me keep him.

"Was there anything you wanted me to change in there?" The merchant asked, opening the dressing room.

"Go bonkers, I trust you," I smiled.

"You do?"

"Why not?" I shrugged.

With a small grin, the merchant turned to the room and released a big puff of air that changed everything into a solid colour with a random design.

"I'll be right back," I said over my shoulder to Raiden before slipping into the backroom.

I won't bore you with a near hour long fashion show, so after a few lengthy outfit changes and stuttering statements from Raiden, I was about to pack up and take what I wanted, but one last item caught me.

Hmm, I don't usually like that colour, but...

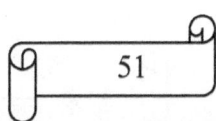

I put my normal outfit back on, folded up the clothes, and took down the hat that I inexplicably was interested in. Once I stepped out of the dressing room, the merchant took the clothes from me and looked through all the merchandise I wanted to take home.

"Last one, I swear," I promised Raiden, showing off my hat. "Thoughts?"

On my head, leaning on the portion of my head that had my bare skin was a magenta beret with an obsidian hexagon badge on the front.

"I think it just matters what you think of it, Corbé," Raiden said softly.

"Well, I think if it was warm I wouldn't wear much more," I adjusted the hat with a giggle.

"Uh…" Raiden's cheeks resumed their blushed state that almost matched my beret.

"It's an expression, Rai," I punched Raiden teasingly. "How much is all this?" I asked the merchant.

"Nothing for you," The merchant shook his head.

"Come on, this stuff is awesome. You need to get *something* for it," I said.

I reached into my cape pocket to bring out the money. Running a few calculations through my head, I decided to round up on all of his wares.

"Here," I handed the merchant a large bundle of black paper bills.

After counting the money, the merchant looked at me in confusion.

"Ms…. This is too much for-"

"Corbé," I smiled as Raiden took up the clothing to place in our personal fabric bags. "Call me Corbé."

"Danke… Corbé," The merchant graciously bowed to me, delicately tensing his grip on his well-earned money.

"I'm so sorry, I got caught up in all of this stuff. What's your name by the way?" I asked the merchant.

"My name is Valentin," The merchant said. "Valentin Piccolo."

"Huh… Valentin," I said. "Like Valentine."

"What's a Valentine?" Raiden asked, placing my bags on the ground so to conserve his strength.

"Seriously? With all the holidays you lot have, you don't have Valentine's Day?" I looked to Raiden and Valentin who both shrugged. "That won't do at all. Give me a tic."

I walked speedily to the centre of the Quad and climbed up the chimaera fountain to address all of Dolorous.

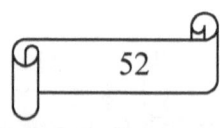

"Hear ye, hear ye, Dolorous! First of all, how's everyone's Merchant Week going?" I asked with everyone cheering happily. "That's fantastic, because this week's gonna be extra special this year. I think it's time you lot learn a bit of a Terrace tradition. It's called Valentine's Day!"

Everyone who looked up at me held confused stares up at their local chancellor.

"It's a day dedicated to love, friendship, and everything happy in the world and that's what we're going to celebrate at the end of the week. In fact…" My mind traced back to my grand entrance and the memory of everyone having so much fun. "*On* Valentine's Day, I'm holding a royal ball and everyone's invited! The one condition: Everyone who attends has to dance. Bring a date if you like or find a date at the ball! Love is love and I love you, Dolorous, so spread it around!"

With cheers and applause resounding around me, I dropped off of the fountain and rejoined Raiden and Valentin.

"So," Raiden rubbed the back of his neck. "Valentine's Day is all about love?"

"That's right," I nodded. "It's one of the better holidays from my home Realm. It was usually when my foster siblings took it a tad easier on me. Not all too much, but still. You better come and you better dance, mister," I winked at Raiden as I walked off to see if I could find any jewellry to go with my new clothes. "Bye, Valentin! Hope to see you at the ball!"

"Bye, Corbé!" Valentin waved goodbye as he watched Raiden and I leave.

"See you, Valentin," Raiden tried to wave goodbye, but failed due to the weight of my shopping bags.

"See you," Valentin nodded.

He looked down at the wad of money that was still in his hands as a smile drew itself upon his vague face.

Next to the booth that I was looking at, Raiden glanced at a pear figured woman in an old-fashioned baker's outfit manning a stand called Aderyn Confections. If you're keeping track of names, you'll recognise 'Aderyn' as Raiden's last name, making it his family's booth that was run by the always cheery and forever pleasant Gladys Aderyn. Currently, she was tying up a few pastry baskets for a collection of customers practically throwing bills into her register.

"Oi, mum," Raiden gently placed my bags down so he could speak to Gladys without strain. "Can I talk to you for a second?"

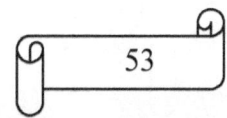

"What about, hon?" Gladys asked, placing a 'Taking Five' sign on the front of her booth as she stepped away to speak with Raiden.

"Uh, just something private," Raiden said.

"Is that so?" Gladys laughed, a knowing smirk on her lips.

Once Gladys and Raiden were at the chimaera fountain, Gladys sat down on its edge with a poised eyebrow and folded arms.

"So, what 'private' matter about Corbé is it this week?" Gladys asked.

"H-how did you-?"

"You do this thing where you have a minimum of seven metres of space before you think it's safe to talk about someone behind their back," Gladys giggled.

"Huh," Raiden scratched his chin. "It should probably be changed to 'out of earshot' now that I think about it."

"Out with it," Gladys tried to refocus her son.

"Corbé's royal ball," Raiden said.

"Ah," Gladys laughed. "You want her to be your date, don't you? So why not?"

"Why not? Because, I'm a bundle of nerves and Corbé's... Corbé. You know how she is. She's cool, she's confident, and she's-"

"Are you mad?!" I blurted in disgust. "5,000 Phlorin? And that's *50%* off? No, thank you."

I placed the ruby necklet on the booth table to move onto the next one over.

In a failed attempt to retain their most recent customer, the merchant called out, "But my queen-"

"And I'm not queen!" I spat over my shoulder.

"Hot tempered," Raiden said in a half-fearful, half-admirative state.

"Always the sugar coater," Gladys ruffled Raiden's hair.

As the Aderyns watched me walk away, Gladys squinted.

"Is Corbé taller than usual?" Gladys asked. "And... plumper?"

"Plumper?" Raiden asked with a tinge of a blush. "I-if you want to phrase it that way, I guess," His hand returned to the back of his neck. "Do you have any tips for me? Like relationship advice?"

"Mayyybe," Gladys placed a finger on her chin. "*But* you're going to have to make tomorrow's batches for the booth."

"Deal," Raiden nodded without hesitation.

"The first step is to be confident, kind of like Corbé. She doesn't care what people think of her, she just does what Corbé does. People love her for that. Be confident, but don't be arrogant. Test it out on

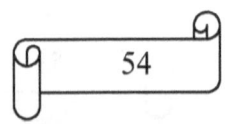

some of the merchants around town. If you manage to haggle down a price then you know it's working."

"Hmm, it's worth a shot, I suppose. Thanks, mum," Raiden gave his mother a warm embrace.

As Raiden went off to go test his 'confidence', Gladys glanced down the way. The man of African descent in all white and orange, Guy, was manning a stand that Gladys wasn't used to seeing, likewise with the products that she was seeing.

"Guy, got a new inventory?" Gladys asked, approaching the booth.

"Just a few miscellaneous objects that I've put together at short notice," Guy said.

Gladys picked up a bronze feather duster, trailing her hand through the metallic vanes.

"These are Snapback's feathers," Gladys said.

"Very perceptive," Guy nodded. "The little bastard sword is taking care of my pub while I'm here. It's another storey for another time."

"You know he's going to be offended by you taking advantage of him," Gladys said.

"Maybe a little," Guy shrugged. "See anything you like?"

"Not that I know of," Gladys gave the items a onceover, placing the feather duster back onto the table. "Unless you can fashion together a flame retardant apron."

"I can do that," Guy took out a notepad and pen to jot down that note.

"Oi, speaking of the little Grinoff," Gladys cast her gaze down the street to see Snapback waddling their way.

"Scrap!" Guy frantically scrambled to collect the items and replace them with a grouping of snow globes he had hidden off to the side. "Hey, Snap, I thought you were taking care of the pub."

"I took care of everything and Harper said she'd watch it for me," Snapback smiled.

"How'd you manage that? I thought she hated you," Guy said.

"She said I was cute for a boy," The Grinoff beamed. "But Gladys," Snapback turned to the baker. "I made you something!"

Snapback reached into his hat to retrieve the friendship bracelet made specifically for Gladys.

"I'm charging hugs for them for Merchant Week," Snapback held the piece of jewellry out with one hand and his other was open for a hug.

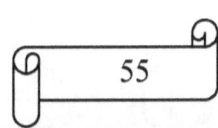

Upon giving the bracelet a closer inspection, Gladys was taken over by a nostalgic and glowing smile.

"D'aww," Gladys cooed. "My son made one just like this when he was five. I love it."

Gladys dropped to her knees and squeezed the Grinoff tightly.

"Ouch," Snapback squawked. "You're really strong, you know that?"

"I used to be a Gryphon Jouster; I've got the bones of a fighter," Gladys winked, beating her clavicle proudly.

She wrapped the bracelet around her wrist and flaunted it to Snapback who shared her broad grin.

"I thought Raiden was good with his hands. He made a bracelet that looked like *that*?" Guy asked.

"I didn't say it was Raiden," Gladys spoke softly.

"Ah… My bad," Guy massaged his earring awkwardly.

A bitter-sweet smile was on Gladys' face as she placed a delicate hand on her friendship bracelet.

"Hey, do you two know where Gawain or Alégna are?" Snapback asked.

"They-"

"I don't know," Guy interrupted Gladys. "Why don't you ask Corbé? She's super clever, right?"

"Ooh, you're right!" Snapback said as he toddled over to me.

"I'll go with you," Gladys said, trailing behind the Grinoff.

With a grumble of his stomach and the scent of cheesy food in the air, the little Grinoff veered off to the side.

"I'll be right back, I'm hungry!" Snapback said before waddling away.

"What is with you lot and these outrageous prices?" I scoffed, moving further down the line of jewellry booths.

"Hmm, 900," Gladys looked at the bracelet I was moaning over. "That's not *that* bad of a price, you know, Corbé."

"You'd think I'd get a discount or something, after all I *am* queen."

"I thought you didn't like being called 'queen'," Gladys reminded me.

"Whatever. Princess prices would be nice," I said.

"It's possible that 'Princess prices' are more expensive. People assume that you're rich," Gladys said.

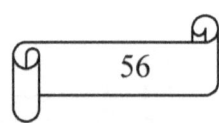

"Just because I am doesn't mean I'm going to be spending all my money at five booths for the entire week," I folded my arms. "And where's Raiden? He's supposed to be carrying my bags."

I searched the Quad for my adviser without a hint of where he'd gone to.

"Hi, Corbé!" Snapback pitched behind me with a calzone in hand that he purchased.

"Hey, Snapback," I said, an instant smile replacing my annoyed scowl. "How's my favourite Grinoff?"

"Good as good," Snapback said, tapping his fist to mine.

"Did you buy that?" I looked to the Grinoff's lunch.

"Yeah! Guy gave me a bunch of Phlorin for helping him around the bar," Snapback beamed, reaching into his pocket to pull out a handful of silver coins.

"Huh, I didn't even know Guy was hiring," I said.

"Me neither," Snapback shrugged.

"I didn't even know he believed in paid help," Gladys added.

"Me neither!" Snapback squawked.

"Who else do you need to give friendship bracelets to?" I asked, trying to peer underneath Snapback's cap.

"Let me see," Snapback peeked into his hat. "I have one for Cath, I have one for Paul, I have one for Black Silver, and I have one for Lotl."

"That's grea-" My amused smile disappeared at the mention of my late friend.

Time for that enlightenment I was speaking of earlier...

A month ago, the woman who introduced me into the wonderful world of Dolorous was someone known as Lotl. She was the Lady of the Lava and she was my caretaker far before I knew it as a fact. I didn't know for how long, but I felt like it might've been for all my life. Lotl devoted her entire existence to protecting me and making sure that I would one day be prepared to take my rightful place as queen. However, on my journey to locate the blood of the original Questing Beast, Merloque, Lotl made the ultimate sacrifice for me. She saved my life in exchange for her own. The mere mention of her name made my heart sink precipitously.

"Snapback..." I spoke with strain. "You *do* know that Lotl's-"

"Oi," Gladys interrupted to speak to Snapback. "Don't you think you should give Alégna and Gawain their friendship bracelets?"

"Right! Where are they?" He asked, searching the Quad.

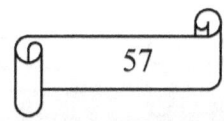

"They're vacationing in Wakalolo," I said sombrely. "It's a Polynesian island in Terrace."

"Ooh, tropical!" Snapback perked. "I'll be right back!"

Snapback leapt in the air and dove hands first with the sound of a chainsaw. He punched his way through the ground and sped off, his burrow trail leading Westward.

"Does Snapback not know?" I asked Gladys.

"I guess it's possible," Gladys said, poising her hand on her chin and her index finger over her upper lip in what I called the 'Stache of Contemplation'. "I could've sworn he knew, but he seems happy. Let's just not burst his bubble over this. I remember letting Raiden and Pog search for the Flatwoods Monster when they were seven."

"Isn't Snapback like five months old or something?" I asked Gladys.

"Sounds about right."

"So, we're going to tell him in seven years?"

"Tell who what?" Snapback asked as his head burst from the ground in front of us, a green lei around his neck and a yellow hibiscus stuck on his hat.

"Snapback," Gladys nearly jumped. "I thought you were going to give Gawain and Alégna their friendship bracelets."

"I did," Snapback said, squirming out of his burrow and patting it down to become impossibly smooth. "They said they liked them!"

"Wow, you've been getting faster," I said. "Ever think of being a postman?"

"Ms. Le Fay," The merchant from before called to me. "I've found another necklet that would be worth a hundred Phlorin less."

"For the last time, I don't want your jewellry!" I barked ravenously at the merchant.

"Corbé, calm down," Gladys placed a hand on my shoulder.

"No, she needs to stop bugging me," I weaselled myself out of Gladys' grip.

"Are you all right?" Gladys asked, placing a hand on my forehead as if I had a fever. "You're acting a tad odd recently."

"What makes you think that?" I redirected my irritated state towards the Aderyn mother.

"You're usually more tenacious than this," Gladys pointed out.

"Aww, you really think that?" I softened.

"That tears it, I don't care if I have to pay for the appointment, I'm taking you to see Guy," Gladys held my hand to walk me to Guy's booth.

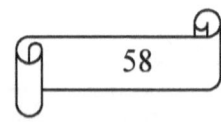

"Why would I need to see Guy?" I asked with a sneer. "There's nothing wrong with me."

"Yep," Guy lowered his stethoscope from my chest and scrawled a few words on his clipboard. "There's something wrong with you."

For the purposes of giving me a look over, Guy sanitised his pub and converted it into a sort of impromptu ER. Thin anti-microbial paper was laid out over all the surfaces, a large magnifying glass was amplifying light towards me from a nearby candle, and Guy used one of my adventure items as a heart monitor. It was a gold and black clawed gauntlet that was usually meant for digging through the ground just like Snapback would. However, he used its pulse sensor ability to assure my vitals were okay.

"What do you mean?" I removed the mercury thermometre from under my tongue. "I feel just fine."

"Well, you *are* just fine," Guy said. "Your weight, your hormonal imbalance, your pulse, and even your height is A-Okay for a healthy maturing thirteen-year-old."

"I'm twelve," I corrected, placing the thermometre on Guy's tool table.

"What's wrong with her then?" Gladys asked, stepping up to my side.

"Nothing is wrong," I said, dropping from the table and going over to retrieve my things. "I already told you. Pay up for the visit."

"You know I don't charge you, right?" The good doctor asked.

"Corbé, you can't pretend that nothing's up," Gladys said, placing a firm hand on my cape to stop me from putting it back on.

"You heard Guy, I'm healthy," I said.

"Eh, for a thirteen-year-old," Guy flipped through his notes.

"I'm twelve," I repeated irritably.

"No, Corbé, you're really not," Guy said, walking over to the table Gladys and I were at.

"What's that supposed to mean?"

"It's supposed to mean," Guy placed my physical results on the table. "you're thirteen-years-old."

Gladys and I glanced at each other before the Aderyn mother released my cape to reach for Guy's clipboard instead.

"Carbon levels, oestrogen, pubescent hormones…" Gladys listed off, looking over my results. "That explains the sudden growth spurt."

"And the mood swings," Guy said.

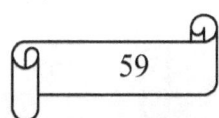

"How can I be thirteen years old? I *am* twelve," I said.

"According to the universe, you're twelve, yes," Guy nodded. "*but* according to your biology, you're thirteen."

"Yeah, but how?" I plopped myself on a seat, waiting for an adequate answer.

"This is only starting now, right?" Gladys tried to clarify.

"Yeah," I said.

"Maybe it has something to do with the fact that you're in Dolorous. Sometimes different Realms affect people the longer they stay. It could just be a side-effect of you being here."

"Accelerated ageing?" I said in disgust. "How much am I going to age? How fast? Am I going to be middle-aged by the end of the week?"

"According to the charts," Guy took back his clipboard from Gladys. "it appears that from here on you're going to age one year every day."

"What?!" I stood up in my shock. "A year per day?! That means I only have, like, two months until I need a walker!"

"Fear not," Guy placed a calming hand on my shoulder. "I can brew up something to suppress the ageing process."

"How soon?" I asked.

"It'll take about…" Guy ran some calculations in his head, taking a few steps back to distance himself from me. "… two days."

"Two days?!"

"Inside voice, Corbé," Gladys urged. "You're yelling quite a lot."

"Two days?" I lowered my voice.

"It's either you stay a fifteen-year-old or you get used to the idea of that walker you were talking about," Guy justified.

"Fine," I sighed. "Could you get to work on that right away? I need to go train with Black Silver."

"Right away, cap'n," Guy saluted.

"Gladys," I turned to the Aderyn mother. "Can you make sure that Lancelot and Opal get food?"

"Sure thing," Gladys nodded. "I'll try to help Guy as much as possible with his brew."

"Thanks, you both," I said in a bittersweet tone.

I gave the two of them quick hugs and headed on my way for my nightly training.

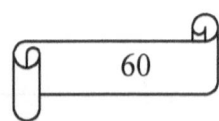

"500! If you don't like it then get lost, Aderyn!" A merchant barked at Raiden who had spent the last ten minutes trying to bargain for a price with a fountain pen salesman.

"Fine, be that way!" Raiden shouted back at the merchant. "Good luck finding Flaxenrose 'cause you know the Aderyns aren't going to make'em for you!"

With a scoff, eye roll, and folded arms, Raiden turned away to clear his mind.

"How does Corbé make it look so easy?" Raiden asked himself.

"It's probably because it *is* easy for her," Valentin said, placing his sign on his booth so that he could take a break. "You're talking about confidence, ja?"

"Yeah. That's the third merchant I'm probably never going to be doing business with anymore," Raiden sighed.

"I wish I could give you some advice on the topic, but I'm not that all confident either. I couldn't even believe that Corbé actually wanted any of my stuff."

"You seemed to get more comfortable when you saw Corbé liked your merchandise."

"Well, ja. No one really understood my passion for tailoring until she came around," Valentin smiled.

"She did the same for me," Raiden chuckled. "I was super into the science and mathematics of magic. Pog used to let me blather away about it, but he never really understood or was interested in it. He just did it to be supportive."

"And Pog would be…?" Valentin poised the question.

"Pog? You don't know Pog? Huh, I thought everyone knew Pog," Raiden said before giving a shrug. "He was the vice-captain of the Blues when he was a Jouster… he was also my brother."

"Ah, well, I'd like to meet him one day," Valentin said.

"You'd be pretty hard-pressed to do so," Raiden massaged his finger that sported his golden ring. "The fact of the matter is that when Corbé came around she was the first person to be legitimately interested in what I liked. Although I don't believe it, Corbé calls herself a bigger nerd than me."

"Hmm," Valentin thought for a moment. "Maybe confidence comes more from being in your element. How about playing by your strengths? You say you're a nerd, why not try a nerd solution?" He gave a shrug.

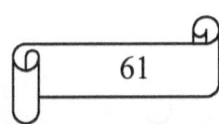

"That actually doesn't sound like a bad idea," Raiden grinned. "Thanks, Valentin."

Raiden glanced down the way to see a fairly busy booth that was selling ancient and newly produced magical relics.

"Now then," Valentin said, stepping up to Raiden's side, his rat joining him on his shoulder. "What was that Flaxenrose stuff you were yelling about earlier?"

With the desire to clear my mind, to have someone to talk to, and to shed a few inches off my new waistline, I sprinted as fast as possible on my run to Black Silver's lesson for the day. When I saw my master coming into focus, I skidded across the dirt to land myself right in front of him.

"Hey, Master Silver," I said with barely a pant in my voice.

"Apprentice Corbé," Black Silver arched a brow to me. "Mine apprentice be quite more mature. Art thou feeling all right?"

"Yeah, about that," I folded my arms as I feverishly beat my heel in the dirt. "According to Guy, I'm ageing at an accelerated pace so by the end of our training you'll be mentoring a cadaver."

"'Tis not uncommon amongst thine lineage, Apprentice Corbé," Black Silver said.

"How do you mean?"

"Morgan Le Fay, thine ancestor, once had a likewise symptom," Black Silver said, approaching me and placing the back of his hand delicately on my birthmarked cheek. "She aged far faster than any other Dolorean, but 'tis merely nigh a curse. 'Tis a symbol of thine importance to the world. Thou art linked to time and it presents itself with thine age."

"So, I have some kind of connexion to time?" I asked quizzically.

"Aye. There be others like thee, some may peer into previous events or put a stopper on motion," Black Silver said.

"There are people out there that can perceive the past and pause time and I get stuck with becoming an old lady?" I rolled my eyes. "Cheers."

"All fortunes happen upon the ones that they see fit," Black Silver said, going back to his starting position to prepare himself for our training session.

"I hope I'm fit then," I rolled my shoulders as Rudy placed my mason jar at my feet. "What's on today's schedule?" I asked as I took up my jar.

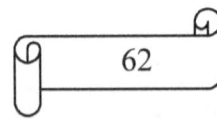

"Thou art going to conduct thine last Light Spectrum power, the power of Life," Black Silver stated. "The power to breathe life into an object or even a mortal be a delicate craft. It requires the greatest care and love towards thine object of desire or the deepest respect or connexion."

"Is it safe to assume that if I have a strong connexion with the 'object' the link will be stronger?" I asked.

"Aye. Thou art familiar with a certain technique in this craft. Spirit Healing," Black Silver said, picking up a few nearby twigs and placing them at his feet.

Back when I fought Lancelot in my Joust, Rudy and I took a few brutal hits. However, by the time all things were said and done, we shared enough of a link to heal each other just by our close contact with one another. That was essentially what Spirit Healing was. Basically, Black Silver was asking me to conduct the same sort of magic... but with a flame?

"No offence to you, Master Silver, or Rick, but I'm not really attached to this thing," I dangled the mason jar by its lid.

"Thou art to animate thine flame before thine lesson may conclude," Black Silver said. "'Tis a delicate magic, Apprentice Corbé. One that requires discipline of the mind as well as thine magic. If it assists thine comprehension, think of it merely as breathing life into thine flame. Like one would do to their own child."

Hmm, breathing life into a flame, huh? I arched a brow as I removed the lid off of my mason jar.

Black Silver motioned for me to approach the twig pile so I assumed he wanted me to place Rick there while I attempted to bring it to life. Like a dense gas, the flame toppled out of the jar to ignite the small collection of wood.

"Okay, *breathing* life," I took a moment to think.

'Like one would do to their own child.' Whatever that means.

I stared into the crackling tendrils of the flame as I tried to determine what my course of action would be.

Just be delicate with it, I told myself.

Slowly, I drew a heart shape in midair and added the cross pattern to finish it up. With the gentlest touch, I tapped the Spell which launched it wildly at the flame causing it to shatter prematurely. It was as if the Spell blew up against an invisible barrier that told me that I did it wrong.

"Persist," Black Silver added his token of motivation.

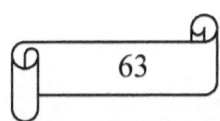

Spells aren't delicate, I thought. *They just fire off the second someone touches it…*

"Hmm?" Black Silver raised a brow, clearly noticing the thought that had crossed my mind.

They fire off when touched… so what if I don't touch it?

This time when I created the Life Spell, I chose to not tap it. Instead, I let it hover for a moment before kissing my finger tips and blowing a kiss in the Spell's direction. The Spell travelled on the light wisp of breath I produced and it found itself in the epicentre of the flame.

"Heh," Black Silver folded his arms in quiet approval.

I was going to ask whether or not it worked, but I noticed something odd about the Spell. It glowed and dimmed in a pulsating fashion, like it was beating like a real heart. A sort of soot-like cocoon wrapped itself around the heart as it sprouted branches. Using the fire and cinders, the heart had grown into a humanoid figure with a ponytail and wings of flame, colour changing skin, and black metal armour that exposed her thighs and had claws and greaves. The pointy nosed and pointy eared Pixie looked to me with a quizzical stare.

"Uh…" I stood up straight as I sustained awkward eye contact with the animated flame. "'Ello," I waved.

The Pixie waved at me in a mimic before standing up and dusting the ashes off of her armour.

"Congratulations," Black Silver said. "I believe thee dubbed her Lady Rick, aye?"

With the utterance of her name, the Life Spell animated flame placed her hands on her hips with an unamused scowl.

Great, my first kid and it already has an attitude, I thought.

"Yeah, her name's Rick," I said with an obvious sting towards my Pixie spawn.

"Then Lady Rick and thee shall meet tomorrow and continue thine lessons together. Sprites enjoy partaking in sugar plums for all meals and drinking nectar. Good night, Apprentice Corbé," Black Silver nodded to Rick and me before walking off.

"Sugar plums? Really?" I asked the Sprite.

With an eye roll, Rick bit her thumb at me and walked over to her jar to sit cross-legged and facing away. I placed the lid on the jar and turned it so that my Sprite would look at me.

"You're really tempting me to shake this thing," I scolded Rick before strapping my wind visors onto Rudy and myself.

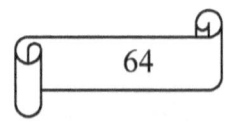

Despite my threat, I safely secured the Sprite onto Rudy's saddle so we could fly back to the castle.

Man, this week is turning out a tad odder than I was expecting. Merchant Week, a runaway Fiend, I created life and... Hold on a tic!

I pulled back on the handles on Rudy's new saddle to bring her to a halt, her hovering in the air above the Kingdom.

I need to find a place to hold the royal ball! Great, Corbé, now you have to deliver or else everyone's going to think you're a sham, I groaned mentally as I veered Rudy away from the castle we nearly made it to.

Instead of heading straight to bed, I decided to take Rudy down the scenic route. As I passed over the Kingdom of Dolorous, I mentally tried to fit everyone into the area with appropriate spacing to dance in pairs.

"Scrap," I mumbled to myself, removing my helmet as if it'd help me think better.

The problem with Dolorous was that since we had a shortage on supplies for aeons we sort of clustered everything tightly together. The most space that we had was the Quad, but that was already preoccupied.

The Withered Woods was too thick and dangerous, Marina's Water Mass was still a sore territory to delve into, the Utmost Underground was a trash pile essentially, and the Bastorial Caves were controlled by a glass Gryphon that wasn't really a fan of mine. On top of all that, the foyer of the palace was preoccupied being the Chamber of Champions.

"Great," I slowed down Rudy's speed so I could clear my mind as we glided. "Wait a minute..."

I dipped my hand into my cape to retrieve the book I always kept close by. It was a silver storybook journal called the Lightitome that had black tank tape partially wrapped over the cover. On its surface was written 'The Forces of Light' in an elegant script, but the title wasn't the part that I was interested in.

After flipping through the book for a while, I discovered the passage I only vaguely recalled. It was in a chapter called 'The Secret Cathedral'.

"Morgan," Arthur beckoned from the doorway of mine chamber.

In his royal silver cloak and his black leather boots, Arthur was a ghost in mine eyes. An angel. I reached out to his

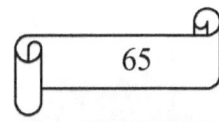

deceivingly warm hand which wrapped around mine. Like following the haunting allure of a will-o-wisp, I trailed behind mine king through the halls and passages of the castle. Despite our descent deeper into the dungeons of the palace the world's heat 'twas sucked away like the breath of coming winter. Darkness shrouded us upon entering the lowest levels of the kingdom. Although swift wafts of wind tingled against mine ankles and the ground beneath mine feet crumbled, I trusted mine king on our way to wherever he was leading me.

With the release of mine hand, the confidence that resided in mine breast retreated my body.

"Arthur," I worriedly spoke in the darkness.

Wordlessly, Arthur bestowed amber light upon the passage we had found ourselves in. Two huge jewel encrusted doors gave way to a beautiful golden room that gave off its own light. The massive room could hold every Dolorean in the kingdom, tenfold. Arches as plentiful as seams in a tunic supported the colossal structure. Every inch of the golden room 'twas etched to be a plentiful and fruitful conglomeration of vegetation. Seemingly endless crystal windows took up the walls that were the source of the unexplainable golden light. Spiral staircases led up high to dozens of levels of balconies that swirled out of mine sight. Floating reflective prisms hovered in the air that refracted the light to every corner of the vast room.

"This place be wondrous," I beamed, my footsteps echoing throughout the hall as I stepped forth towards the centre.

"'Tis, aye," Arthur smiled from behind.

As I turned, I found mine king bowing down to me with an offered palm. The moment I took his hand, he swept me off my feet to dance to only the music that played in our hearts and minds.

Hmm, I thought. *'Every Dolorean in the kingdom, tenfold'*, eh?

"The Secret Cathedral," My lips grew into a smirk as I ran my finger on the silver lining of the page.

Although it was technically the day after, I couldn't wait to start the search for the Secret Cathedral. I whipped out my gold Bluetooth and dialled up Raiden. It took a few redials until finally I heard him moaning over the line.

"Raiden!" I shouted loud enough to wake up my royal adviser fully.

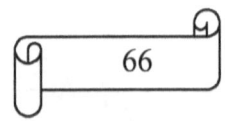

"Corbé," Raiden groaned. "What are you doing? It's not even orange light out."

"Quit your moaning," I ordered him. "I need your help to find the Secret Cathedral."

"The Secret Cathedral? What Secret Cathedral?" Raiden asked, gaining an interested yet still groggy tone.

"It's a room big enough to host the ball I promised everyone," I said. "Apparently, it's in the deepest depths of the castle."

"Huh. And... you want to find that *now*?"

"The sooner the better," I said. "I need more time to shop later."

"Of course," Raiden sighed. "All right. Should I just meet you at the castle gate?"

"Nah, I see your house," I glanced over at the nearby Aderyn Confections. "I'll pick you up. Be right there."

After hanging up and donning my wind visor, I held Rudy's saddle tightly to allow her to do one of her new favourite moves.

"Dive-Bomb!" I shouted.

Rudy angled herself downward with her beak leading directly for the Aderyn household.

Lancelot was usually dead asleep at this time of night, but tonight he was now wide awake. He sat up in his bed, not knowing for what specific reason he woke up. Maybe it was the itch on his nose that he couldn't quite scratch or the footsteps he heard throughout the castle, either way he was up.

The false king rose to give his cell a few good paces. His slow walking quickly turned into short-lived sprints since he only had so much space to work with. Controlled breaths were next to calm his chaotic mind coupled with him taking on the lotus position. In and out, in and out, in and out, in and... slump.

"What am I? A monk?" Lancelot asked himself with annoyance, flumping onto his back with a groan. "You're an athlete, Lance, not a monk."

The ex-king placed his braced hands behind his head and did a quick kip-up to get back onto his feet. He fell forwards, his handcuffs clanking against the ground. With heavy exhales, Lancelot proceeded to do a series of vigorous pushups.

"Fifty-five... Sixty..." Lancelot flicked his hair, getting his sweat out of his tangled mane. "Ninety-Five... One-Hundred..." Although

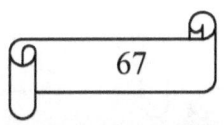

he was exhausting himself, that was the point for him to get back to sleep. "Four-ninety-five... Five... Hundred..."

Just as he was about to undergo his second set, Lancelot looked straight forward. There weren't many things in the dimly lit dungeon, but the one thing that he saw made him slow his frantic pushups until he was just in the plank position. The ex-king's focus was interrupted by the sight of our shared unfinished chess game.

After a while of him blankly staring at the game board, he pushed himself off of the ground and back onto his feet. With a few wipes of his brow and one final long drawn breath, Lancelot went straight back to sleep.

"You know, waking someone up could be a lot quieter than crashing into their bedroom," Raiden said.

"Sorry," I shrugged. "Rudy was excited and when she makes that face I can't stop her. I'll help you patch up the roof."

"I'm holding you to that," Raiden half-heartedly threatened with a yawn.

In the start of our search for the Secret Cathedral, I brought Raiden and I down to the lowest level of the castle. Currently, we were standing at the foot of the stairs just before entering what I'd imagine Hell would look like to those with automatonophobia. Literally, it was an entire floor of the castle dedicated to nothing but stone statues. They were all arranged in a giant circle facing towards the walls. Every statue was of a prominent figure in Dolorean history holding their weapon or item of choice. I could pick out a few that I knew for sure. There was Balin with his staff, Lancelot with his standard Gryphon Jousting Lance, and Tes with her lute.

"This is *totally* not serial-killery," Raiden mumbled, inspecting a spear wielding mermaid lounging in a shallow pool.

"According to the book, the key to opening the path to the Secret Cathedral is love," I said, pulling out the Lightitome.

"Love?" Raiden arched his brow with his cheeks progressively gaining a pink pigment. "H-how's that?"

"Morgan says that there are three riddles that link up to these statues. Basically, all we have to do is move the statues towards the centre and make them face the ones that share true love."

"W-what are the riddles, e-exactly?" Raiden asked, peeking over my shoulder.

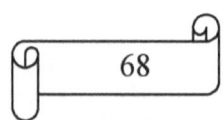

"That's the spirit," I bumped my hip against Raiden's. "Riddle number one: 'From light and dark, love 'tis ne'er apart. Against the heat of war, no one may ever ask for more.'"

"Light and Dark…" Raiden adjusted his glasses as he trailed around the room to look over the statues. "How punny do you think Morgan was?"

"Well, she came up with the term Egg-Plant to describe the plant that a Grinoff hatches from," I tabbed the chapter that I referenced as I continued to skim over the riddles. "So, I'm assuming *very* punny."

"This is Darque," Raiden pushed the statue he was standing in front of towards the centre.

It was a full-figured pirate woman with wildly messy short hair, an eye patch, knee high boots, a multi-pocketed and buttoned frock coat, and hoisted a shotgun skyward.

"She was one of the Light Force Generals during the War of Utopolous."

"I've read about her, she's feisty," I giggled, admiring the statue for a bit too long.

"Oookay," Raiden said. "As far as I recall, she was in love with…" He walked around the room to locate Darque's true love. "Corsair."

If Darque was to the West, then Corsair's statue was to the South. Like Darque, Corsair was dressed like a pirate. She was in more of a lunging position with her flintlock pistol pointed forward. A smug grin was on her face half of which was covered in gauze and she had more than a dozen pistols holstered into her waistcoat.

"All right, let's face these pretty ladies towards each other," I placed the Lightitome on the floor to grab Darque so Raiden could handle Corsair.

It was simple to shift the statues, thankfully, and when that was done we could hear a series of clicks just beyond the walls of the chamber.

"Sweet," I dusted off my hands. "Now, onto the second riddle."

"Hey, Corbé," Raiden rubbed his neck awkwardly as he approached me. "I was wondering something…"

"'Under the sea, that's where she'll be. Cogs and springs, with loving feelings'," I recited. "Marina!"

I stepped over to the mermaid statue and pushed it to the centre.

"Yeah, Marina," Raiden sighed.

"Do you see another Mermaid around here?" I asked.

"Let me check," Raiden said, going back to search. "Well, there aren't any Mermaids, but 'Cogs and Springs' could mean this one."

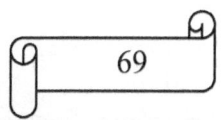

I joined Raiden's side to see the statue was of the mad inventor, Faberge. It was a high likelihood that Raiden modelled his look after him. He wore a waist coat, slacks, a dress shirt rolled up to the elbows, but had a monocle that dangled from around his neck in replacement to Raiden's glasses. Features-wise, he had fire-like hair, a button nose, and a scraggily beard that encompassed his deranged smile.

"Aww," I gawked at the thought of Marina being in love with Faberge.

Mermaids weren't necessarily fond of males, but I suppose that was just a recent development. As we directed Faberge towards Marina, more tumblers unlocked.

"One last one," I said, referring to the book one last time. "Riddle number three: 'My warrior so brave, my love to his grave. My darling so strong, we shall meet again anon.'"

"That book was written by Morgan, yeah? So, isn't that just King Arthur?"

"Pretty much."

I tucked the Lightitome away so that we could approach the first king and queen of Dolorous.

Morgan was in a long dress with a shepherd's staff in one hand and an outstretched beckoning gesture preoccupying the other. A gesture that seemed eerily similar to Valaeria's peculiar handshake she had me do. The Queen had her hair in a long braid that went to the middle of her back and had my birthmark on her face. Or rather I had *her* birthmark on *my* face.

"'Ello, gram-gram," I smiled to my ancestor before getting a good grip on her.

I shoved Morgan into place and posed her in the direction of where I saw King Arthur's statue was. Raiden did the same for the armour wearing and sword flaunting king and rotated him to face his wife. And... well...

"Uh," Raiden looked at the two statues in confusion. "Is something supposed to be happening?"

"It *should*," I said. "Give me a sec," I pulled out the book again. "'My warrior so brave, my love to his grave. My darling so strong, we shall meet again anon.' Morgan was in love with King Arthur... Right?"

"Well..." Raiden's face contorted as a thought passed through his mind.

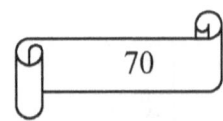

"Well what?" I looked up from the book to the awkward looking Aderyn son.

"When I was young, my mum told me that love... it's complicated. There are three loves that exist in this world. One is your first love that you stay in love with, one is your true love that you find by chance, and one is the..." Raiden glanced at the statues of Morgan and Arthur. "The love you end up with... no matter how much you aren't meant to be with them."

"Are you saying...?"

In the Lightitome, it seemed so convincing that Morgan was in love with King Arthur. They shared the castle, they danced, and they were married for goodness sake!

But now that I think about it... I searched the room for a particular statue I had in mind. *There was one other man in Morgan's life...*

"'My love to his grave,'" I reminded myself of the verse.

On the opposite side of the room stood a tall statue in skeletal armour that held a scythe and Morgan's same outstretched arm as if it called to her.

"Catlon," I stood in front of the magician. "The first Grim Reaper."

Personally, I shipped Morgan and Catlon more intensely than Morgan and Arthur, but it was odd knowing that she felt the same way too. Even more so that she never ended up with the one she *really* wanted to be with.

"You were always my favourite," I whispered to the Reaper. "Put Arthur away," I hollered to Raiden. "This is Morgan's man."

Raiden pulled Arthur's statue back into place so that I could replace it with Catlon's. Once the statue was positioned and facing his love, the far wall almost immediately opened up as if eager to show off the room beyond. The jewel encrusted doors from the storeybook were revealed. After pushing them open, the golden room from the book was just as Morgan described it.

"Yes! Success!" I whooped. "Now all we have to do is get this place prepared for the end of the week. I can see it."

I poised my hands in a rectangular fashion so I could envision placements of temporary party furniture.

"Drink table on one side, snack table on the other so that people are forced to walk around and mingle," I said. "I can set up a podium right there for announcements. We could get Guy's karaoke night buddies to play some music."

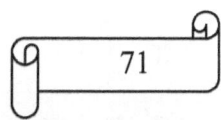

"Snapback found a drum set in the Utmost Underground," Raiden added. "Maybe he can play with the band."

"Yeah!" I beamed excitedly. "You know how to dance, right?" I glanced over to Raiden.

"I've been to a few balls before," Raiden said.

That doesn't really answer my question.

"This'll be fun!" I perked. "We're going to have to cover up those statues so to not scare off the kids, but other than all of that it should be good to go!"

"Great," Raiden yawned. "We can go to sleep now, right?"

"Dismissed," I saluted him with an eyeroll.

"Thanks, but I'll walk you out," Raiden gestured for me to join his side.

"What a gentleman," I laughed.

Even though I was excited for the Valentine's Day Ball, I was still susceptible to tiredness. As I walked alongside Raiden towards the exit away from the Secret Cathedral, my eyelids started to get heavy.

"So, Corbé," Raiden fiddled with his ring. "I was wondering... did you have a date to the ball yet?"

"No," I yawned. "I've been busy."

"Interesting. And were you planning on finding a date *at* the ball?"

"Possibly," I placed my hand over my mouth to suppress a second sigh of fatigue.

"Well, if you want, we could-"

The sound of my body thudding to the ground halted Raiden's words. Although I had plenty of energy a moment ago, sleep seemed to seduce my body near instantly. I curled up with my hands snuggly tucked under my cheek as if the stone floor was a marshmallow level pillow. A bittersweet smile happened upon Raiden's face when he looked at me.

"Thank God," Raiden said with relief.

Carefully, the Aderyn son picked me up and cradled me close so he could take me to my bedroom.

"I was so not ready to ask you out," Raiden admitted.

As he walked up the several flights of stairs to the highest point in the castle, I nestled myself against Raiden's chest.

No, Raiden. No, you weren't.

The moment I woke up, before I put on my makeup, I decided to test out my new purchases from the Quad. From a friendly merchant in

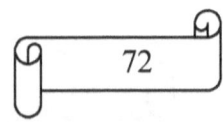

town, I got an acoustic guitar which he personally tuned for his majesty herself. In addition, he threw in a few guitar picks as a bonus. They were cheap and thin plastic, but hey, they were free.

In front of me on my bed was a legal pad and a quill-pen that I was writing my current song with. As I lightly played, I cleared my throat and strummed slowly in order to make sure I was getting each note right.

"Trials by fire, driven by desire, my dreams and hopes only get bigger and higher," I sang softly, readjusting my fingers carefully in between verses. "Wheeling through the sky, I try and I try, kissing all my worries and fears goodbye," I beat my guitar as I progressed onward. "Friends by my side… my flock has arrived… we will glide on the winds of the rising… tide!" My voice cracked on the high note in the ugliest fashion imaginable. "Ugh," I recoiled in disgust. "I'm not in love with that."

I decided to place my guitar into a corner, tuck my legal pad away, and pretend that that hadn't happened. Although I was completely prepared to forget about that fail of a high note, Rick wasn't. She was grumpily woken up by my singing since she was only two metres away in her jar on my chest of drawers.

"Get used to it, girly, I'm a song bird," I waved away the pissy face that Rick was giving me.

With my morning music session spoiled for myself, I moved onto getting ready. I decided that I didn't really care if anyone saw my birthmark and went natural today. Once my hair was 'done', I went to my cupboard to try on some of Valentin's clothes.

I had a miniature heart attack when I felt that I couldn't fit into my new cardigan, but something happened which put my heart at ease. The threads and seams of the cardigan unfurled, grew, and then laced themselves back together to form a size that actually fit me.

I am so *over Tes' clothes,* I smirked as I finished getting dressed. *Although...* I glanced over at my adventuring gear and then shook myself out of the tiny depression I found myself delving into. *You'll get your chance eventually.*

"What do you think? Does it look good?" I asked, facing the Sprite who was barely paying attention. "Oi, only person in the room with me," I tapped the glass. "I asked you a question, missy."

Rick glanced over at me only to give a half-shrug.

"Kids," I rolled my eyes.

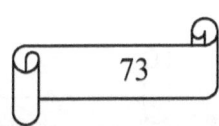

After clipping my cape on, I picked Rick up and placed her delicately into my inner pocket.

"Come on, you ingrate, let's get some breakfast," I said on my way out of my bedroom.

Heading into town, I went directly to Gladys for some nosh. Surprisingly enough, she had a few sugar plums on hand. I didn't really feel like Rick deserved them, but she was stuck in a jar so it sort of levelled out. For me, I chose to have a cocoa banger, a menu item that wasn't well-sold by the Aderyns, but I chose to try it today. I had a craving. A cocoa banger's basically a batter covered Colby cheese filled bratwurst breaded in graham cracker crumbs, drenched in chocolate syrup, and sprinkled with powdered sugar and a bit of ground mustard... I repeat... I had a craving.

I purchased a second one and made my way to the end of the Quad to meet up with Valentin.

"Morning, Val," I greeted the merchant as he was setting up shop.

"G-good morning, Ms.... Corbé," Valentin laughed to himself. "What brings you by?"

"Just saying hi to a friend," I said. "You want one?"

I offered the second cocoa banger to Valentin.

"What in Earth is this thing?" Valentin took the dessert from me and inspected it for a moment.

"It's breakfast! Tuck in!" I insisted, taking a bite from mine to show how good I thought it was.

Valentin seemed reluctant at first, but the smile on my face enticed him to try it out for himself. After his first bite, he let all the different flavours settle among his taste buds. As he ate, there was a sort of vague smile on his face coupled with him chuckling at the absurd breakfast item.

"You like it?" I asked.

"I actually do," Valentin laughed.

"I'm glad," I grinned. "Does your friend want some?" I looked over to the rat on Valentin's shoulder.

"Heh, 'friend'," Valentin gave a sombre chuckle as he allowed the rat to nibble a bit of the opposite side of his banger.

"What do you mean by that? Of course, he's a friend. Anyone can be your friend if you give them a chance," I said, patting the rat's head delicately as it ate. "He seems to really like you."

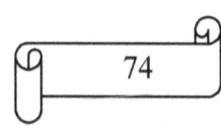

"It's just a rat," Valentin said. "He's just here because he's curious and hungry."

The semi disappointed frown on my face made Valentin reconsider his statement.

"He is good company though," Valentin smiled, stroking the rat's back lightly.

"What's his name?" I asked.

"Hmm," Valentin pondered the rodent's name as it began to clean its whiskers of the molten cheese. "How about Colby?"

"Hehe, I think that's a great name for him," I beamed.

"I hope he remembers it even after I go back home," Valentin said.

Now's my chance for some answers...

"Where *is* your home exactly, Valentin?" I made the question sound as natural as possible. "I don't think I've ever seen you before this week."

Valentin staggered, taking a half-step back.

I dropped my hand off to the side, hiding it behind my thigh and feeding some of my aura into my index and middle fingers just in case this went south faster than I thought it would. Although I trusted Valentin, I also trusted Valaeria and her warnings.

Even though I was battle ready, it was an unneeded precaution.

"I..." Valentin fiddled with the cocoa banger's stick in his hand. "Ja, I'm not from here."

With Valentin's words, I allowed my aura to disperse from my fingertips.

"I come from Shroudolous," Valentin confessed. "I'm what you would call a 'Fiend'. Funny thing about us is that we don't necessarily have clothing per se. All of our wardrobe is decided for us when we're born and it basically becomes our skin. I don't wear this for fashion's sake," The Fiend gestured to his rainbow clothes. "I wear it because I have no other choice."

"It looks good on you," I encouraged. "I don't know many people that can pull off the whole pied look."

"Danke," Valentin laughed. "It's just that when you live in a kingdom that doesn't need clothing, it renders being a tailor meaningless," He sighed. "I never wanted to do anything else other than make clothes and honestly, I'm not good at many things other than tailoring so that's what I came here to do. I heard Merchant Week was going on, so I thought it'd be the perfect time to try my luck. So

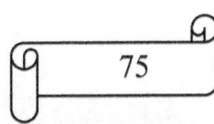

far, you've been my only real customer… and friend… other than Raiden and Colby, I suppose."

Aww, Val, I moped in my head.

"This kingdom has been the same way for aeons," I said. "For the longest time it was ruled over by King Balin, but when I came around it took some time for people to warm up to the idea of a new ruler. Give these people a chance and some time, maybe they'll warm up to you too."

"Hmm…" Valentin looked to the rat on his shoulder, giving him a warm stroke or two. "… maybe."

I didn't know how long it was going off, but when the conversation went silent, I could hear my Bluetooth chirping.

"Oof," I rushed to retrieve and insert the earpiece. "I have to take this, but I hope you two's days go well. Bye, Val. Seeya, Colby," I waved them goodbye.

"Same to you, Corbé," Valentin bowed to me as Colby did the same.

"'Ello, who's this?" I asked.

"It's Raiden," The Aderyn son said over the line.

"Raiden, where've you been? I have half of a cocoa banger with your name on it," I said, turning my breakfast over on its stick.

"Eww, you actually bought one of those things?" Raiden's disgust was tangible to me even over the Bluetooth.

"You know, funny thing, Gladys made the same comment," I giggled. "It's not bad."

"It's not good either," Raiden mumbled. "Anyway, I just need you to approve on my design for the Secret Cathedral."

"Wait, you've been doing that without me?" I halted my walk around the Quad.

"Uhh… Is the wrong answer, 'yes'?"

"Yes," I said firmly.

"Then 'no'."

"Yeah, too late."

"Sorry. I *do* still need help with a few last-minute touches."

"All right, I'll meet you there."

After I got some foil from Gladys to wrap my cocoa banger and pocketed my Bluetooth, I headed back for the castle.

Once an hour or so passed, the business in the Quad started to die down since everyone was going out for brunch. Meanwhile, Valentin

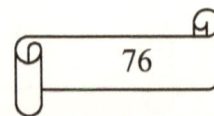

was busy organising his clothes as a man wearing a white pair of Inuit sunglasses approached his stand.

"Give them a chance," Valentin told himself quietly. "Good morning," He greeted the customer warmly. "See anything you like?"

The slit of the man's sunglasses glowed black as he looked at Valentin's chest area.

"Yes, I do," A smirk appeared on the customer's face.

Faster than Valentin or Colby could react, the man drove a strong right cross into Valentin's cheek. Valentin stumbled onto his bum in his sudden daze. The 'customer' leapt over the table and reached into Valentin's tunic. Relieving the merchant of his wad of money, he booked it into a nearby alleyway, however Valentin was unaware of that. He searched the area for the mugger, but he had already escaped.

Colby crawled onto Valentin's left shoulder to inspect the Fiend's new bruise.

"Give them a chance," Valentin scoffed, running his fingers feverishly through his hair and clawing at his scalp. "I mean... just... Gahhh!"

The Fiend beat his fist into the ground, a spark of dark energy bursting from the impact. Valentin should've been angry, he should've chased after the thief, he should've done something, but all he could do was curl himself into a foetal position.

"This was a stupid idea," Valentin griped. "This Kingdom is no better than mine."

With a clenched jaw and a low growl in his throat, Valentin took out his duffle bag. He folded up all of his shirts, trousers, and hats as Colby assisted by placing some gloves into the bag as well.

"You can come if you want," Valentin told Colby. "I don't think you'll like Shroudolous all too much though."

Valentin abandoned his vacant stand to head for the exit of the kingdom as rain started to pour down.

"Heyyy, Raiden," I hollered into the statue infested chamber. "I kind of ate your cocoa banger on the way here, so to make up for it I brought you your favourite drink. Guinebeer!" I sang.

On my way to the Secret Cathedral, I bought two bottles of Guinebeer from the Experience Bar (Guy's pub). It was a red light-beer that was meant for mental stimulation rather than alleviating inhibitions, or at least that's what Guy marketed it as. To be technical,

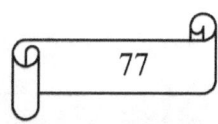

the legal drinking age in Dolorous was thirteen, but to *also* be technical, I was biologically fourteen currently, so…

I pushed open the doors of the Secret Cathedral and almost dropped the beer bottles.

"Looks good?" Raiden asked.

Although the cathedral was beautiful what with the Dolorean fire braziers every few metres to warm the cold room, the buffet tables decorated with ice sculptures of birds, and floating hors d'oeuvre trays that roamed around the area, I wasn't looking at that stuff really. I was looking at Raiden. Raiden gave himself a don haircut, new pair of silver framed rectangular glasses, and wore a black tuxedo with his coin neckpiece.

"Yeah, it looks great," I giggled, walking up to the Aderyn son. "Why haven't I seen this outfit before?"

"Because I just bought it," Raiden said, taking one of the Guinebeers and twisting its cap. "and the haircut. I didn't *buy* the haircut, I *got* a haircut, there's a barber in town, he was nice, didn't talk much, and I'm just going to drink this before I turn this into a run-on sentence," He laughed at himself as he shut himself up by taking a swig of his beer.

"It's a good look for you," I said, taking the cap off of my bottle.

"Hmm," Raiden knit his brows at the sight of me drinking with him.

"It's a long storey," I shrugged as the buzz started up in the back of my head.

"Does it start with 'Corbé does whatever she wants' and ends with a period?" Raiden teased, capping his Guinebeer to place it on one of the buffet tables.

"Let's go with that," I laughed with a wink. "So, what did you need me for? This place looks already ready."

"I was wondering if you wanted the band to play over there," Raiden pointed to one corner opposite to the entrance doors. "or over there," He gestured to the other.

"I don't really know," I said.

"Or we could just not have the band."

"We *need* music, Raiden, it's a ball," I giggled before taking another swig of my Guinebeer.

"Not necessarily," Raiden walked over to me and held his hand out.

He placed my Guinebeer bottle down so he could hold my hand and grab my waist.

Ooh, confident Raiden's out to play today. I like.

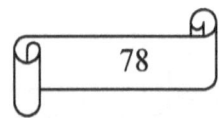

As we moved further down the hall, we partook in an impromptu dance together. We twirled, we trailed down the hall, and Raiden even dipped me to the imaginary music we apparently shared together.

"Wow, Raiden. 'A few balls'?" I asked him with a coy brow.

"Do *not* say that phrase out of context please," Raiden laughed as he spun me out and back in.

"Will do," I giggled.

"So, what're you going to wear for the ball?" Raiden asked, giving me a delightful tango swoop. "Something elegant I'm imaging."

"I don't know. Maybe that dress you seemed to like so much," I said.

"I like you in anything."

O, do you now? No classic Raiden-retraction? 'No, I didn't mean it like that *Corbé.' Maybe I should buy some more Guinebeer.*

"What if I just show up in my adventuring clothes?" I asked.

"That's always been my favourite," Raiden said. "You should consider adding some armour to it though. Something light weight, something that gives a full range of motion, something that's multipurposed, and... gosh..." He placed his forehead on mine as he burrowed his mind in thought. "What colour would it be?"

"I don't really know, Raiden," I bit my lip. "I guess I haven't really thought about it that much."

"I guess you still have time to think about a few things," Raiden said.

"I suppose so."

Raiden eventually slowed our dance to a halt. We separated from each other and stared deeply into one another's eyes.

"Yeah, so," I looked to the left corner of the Secret Cathedral. "What about over there for the band so that we can have that area over there open to access the balconies."

"That sounds like a great idea," Raiden smiled, walking over to the buffet table to retrieve his Guinebeer. "I love balconies."

"And why's that? If you don't mind me asking."

"I never mind," Raiden shook his head before taking a sip of his beer. "I don't know, just that feeling of looking down on the world. Not like I'm a superior, like I can see every piece and every cog of a clock. Everything that makes it tick. Everything that makes it move. Seeing it all just makes me feel so-"

"Connected?" I offered, walking over to Raiden with my drink in hand as well.

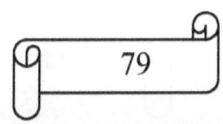

"Exactly. I don't feel so alone anymore."

"Is that why you wanted to be a Gryphon Jouster?"

"*Want*," Raiden corrected.

"Why you *want* to be a Gryphon Jouster?" I bumped my hip to his.

"One of the many reasons," Raiden nodded.

"I guess that decides it," I said. "Left corner it is," I poised my bottle to Raiden so we could toast. "Anything else you need me here for?"

"Just one," Raiden placed his bottle down and faced fully towards me. "Corbé."

"Hmm," I capped my drink before I choked out of shock.

Is he doing what I think he's doing?

"Raiden?" I asked.

"Can I safely infer that you still don't have a date for the ball?"

Are we really doing this?

"You can."

"Well then," Raiden said, gaining a sly smile. "Would you like to go to the Valentine's Day Ball with me?"

Holy Grail. Am I dreaming right now? I internally beamed. *He actually did it.*

"Raiden... I would *love* to go to the Valentine's Day Ball with you," I spoke steadily so to not utter a shrill squeal.

"Can't wait. I'll be putting some finishing touches on this place if you need me," Raiden said.

"Thanks, Raiden."

As I headed out of the Secret Cathedral, I gave him a giddy doubletake.

"Thank *you*," Raiden cheered to me with his bottle before downing the rest of his beverage.

Looks like Raiden and I have a date! Finally! I smiled broadly to myself.

Once he was sure that I had left the Secret Cathedral, Raiden removed a brown leather lariat from his pocket that glowed with a subtle shimmer of silver.

"And thank *you*, 'confidence'," Raiden smirked, tossing the necklace in the air and catching it. "Best purchase I've ever made."

Since I was on the level anyway, I decided to pay a little visit to the ex-king of Dolorous.

"You awake?" I called into the SRO hall.

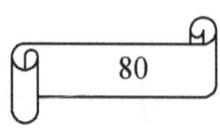

"I'm always awake," Lancelot murmured from inside of his cell. "You pack an umbrella?"

"Why would I?"

I approached Lancelot's cell to find his back facing me, him staring out the window at the rain pouring in the streets of Dolorous.

"Ah," I sat down 'next to' Lancelot and watched the rain with him. "No, but I don't mind it."

"A lot of people think that rain is an omen of coming disaster," Lancelot said, shifting in his sitting position to lay more comfortably.

"And what do you think?"

"Codswallop," Lancelot scoffed. "The world can't detect good or evil, it can just... feel."

"That's not codswallop, because...?"

"White clouds are normal, black clouds bring storms, but grey clouds bring rain. It can drown a village or grow its crops, rain doesn't mean disaster all the time, it merely means change."

We remained in silence, listening to the trickling of the rain. I looked to the chess set that represented the constant battle between Lancelot and me. Since no braziers were lit and only the minimal light coming from outside illuminated the chess set, I couldn't detect the difference in colour between the two shades of game pieces.

"Do you remember the day you overthrew me, Corbé?" Lancelot asked me. His tone wasn't one of sourness, but a tone of nostalgia.

"It was a Hell of a day," I ran my hand across my cheek where Lancelot had slashed me during our Joust.

"Sorry for that," Lancelot said, knowing what I was thinking without a single glance over. "I think we were both a tad miffed that day."

"That's an understatement. Why do you bring it up?" I refocused Lancelot.

"Practically the moment you took over, Dolorous saw its first rain since the dawn of time. Things had changed. I don't think it's beyond my bounds to say that it's too early to tell if it's for better or worse."

Although it sounded like a wanker thing to say, I knew what he meant. Things appeared to be better in Dolorous, but with my arrival it was long said that it would welcome new threats, new enemies, and new powers beyond the confines of just Dolorous. One of these days, Dolorous would be threatened by something I couldn't handle, but that's what all my preparation was for. To be ready for whatever comes my way.

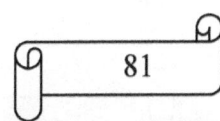

"I have to go train with Black Silver so I can get some rest for the Valentine's Day Ball," I said robotically as I rose to exit the dungeon.

"The what?" Lancelot glanced over his shoulder.

"Valentine's Day, it's a day that-"

"I know what Valentine's Day is. You're throwing a ball?"

"Yeah, it's going to be in the Secret Cathedral tomorrow night," I told Lancelot.

"You know the Secret Cathedral is supposed to be secret for a reason, right?" He asked.

"I kind of figured."

"Did you invite Tes?" Lancelot asked.

"Yes, everyone in Dolorous is invited."

"Good. Make sure she has a fun time."

"I will," I assured him.

On my way out, just before I shut the door to the dungeon, I heard Lancelot say, "O..."

"O, what?" I looked back down the hall.

"You found the Secret Cathedral," Lancelot said.

"Aye," I nodded slowly.

"That means that you know how Morgan felt about Catlon. Love is a fickle thing, Corbé. It's one of the non-physical things in the universe to confirm time is real."

"How's that?"

"Because, time is the only thing that separates a decision to make and a mistake made. Catlon was just too late to speak of his feelings towards Morgan. Don't repeat history, Corbé. Take it from someone who's lived more than his fair share of lifetimes," Lancelot laid himself down to rest. "it's best to live with your heart on your sleeve than in a jar."

"... Good night, Lancelot..." I exited the dungeon to head for my training session.

"Good night, Corbé."

By the time I exited the castle, Guy was outside the front gate with a bronze feather umbrella to shroud me from the rain.

"Such a gentleman," I curtseyed to the bartender.

"Not by much," Guy massaged his chest with a strained face on.

"What does that mean?"

"It's nothing," Guy groaned. "I just sort of need someone to talk to."

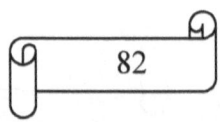

"This is new," I said, opening the gate so we could head down to the Quad. "What's on your mind?"

"If it was you, what would be more important, a good business or, I guess, a good friend?"

"A good friend," I answered automatically. "What kind of question is that?"

"I-I know, I know," Guy ran his hand through his hair. "It's just... I might've done something stupid and well... I don't know..."

"Does it have anything to do with this?" I pointed a finger to the umbrella we were standing underneath. "I can tell these are Snapback's feathers. Did you piss him off?"

"I guess so."

For the past month, I didn't really know Snapback to be one to be mad at someone, but Guy had his ways I suppose. Thinking about that, I looked down at my wrist to the friendship bracelet that the little Grinoff gave me earlier in the week. Glancing over at Guy, I couldn't help but notice the absence of one on his person.

"Do you consider Snapback a friend?" I asked Guy.

"I mean, he's a nice kid/creature... thing, but I'm not necessarily friends with many people around here. It makes lying and conning people out of their money easier," Guy admitted.

"Does Snapback consider *you* a friend?" I reversed the query.

Guy's face fell into a moment of thought, staring at the path in front of us and concentrating on nothing physically tangible.

"Everyone deserves a chance, Guy," I told the merchant. "Snapback is one of the greatest friends someone can have. I think you should really give it some thought to try to fix whatever it is you broke."

"Maybe..." Guy pondered. "I'm sorry I brought it up, it's just that the fellas at the pub don't really take kindly to sob storeys."

"It's okay," I softly punched Guy in his shoulder. "What are friends for?"

As we entered the Quad, it was evident that everyone either had awnings over their booths or were hastily setting them up.

"So, have you made progress on the anti-ageing cream or potion or smoothie or whatever?" I asked Guy.

"Yes, actually," Guy chuckled. "I'm heading to the Quad to retrieve some materials for it with my assistants."

"Cool. Thanks-a-mill, Guy. I can't wait to not have to worry about this anymore... Wait, assistants?"

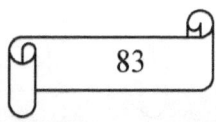

"Speaking of which," Guy gestured to a pair of womanly figures who were at a produce stand.

One was slimmer in red and the other was more full-figured in blue with both of them wearing black hooded ponchos.

That one looks like Gladys and the other is...

"No, no," The lady in red said, taking an apple away from Gladys and replacing it with a bunch of translucent orange berries. "Astrum Berries have deeper magic warding properties."

I know that voice...

"Afternoon, Gladys... Tes," I greeted the ladies.

The two of them turned to me with smiles once they saw who I was.

"Oof, your voice is already getting lower," Tes said.

"Yeah, I almost didn't recognise it," Gladys added.

"What brings you by?" I asked them, Tes immediately picking up on my insinuation.

"When you've been around for as long as I have, you pick up a lot of different talents," Tes said, selecting a few more discoloured fruits and vegetables. "Dancing, singing, alchemy, harnessing quantum energy, and a bit of potion making. I don't know as much as Raiden does, honestly I don't know if *anyone* does, but I dabble."

"Huh, interesting."

I cheated myself away from Tes to murmur to Guy.

"Why *didn't* you get Raiden to help you with this by the way? I'd prefer it," I told Guy.

"Raiden's busy and plus this is a very old potion we're working with, a Grande Brew. It has a lot more rules to it. Old magic can only be negated by old magic and your ageing problem traces way back to Morgan Le Fay. It requires three different potion makers: An Arcane One, a Maternal One, and a Jack One. Nothing more, nothing less. Besides, do you think I would go to Tes if it wasn't absolutely necessary?"

Great, my life is in the hands of Tes... I'm so gonna be an old lady.

"By when do you all think this is going to be finished?" I asked.

"Optimistically..." Gladys thought for a moment.

"We'll have it to you either before or during the Valentine's Day Ball," Tes guesstimated.

"I suppose that'll have to do," I half-shrugged.

As Guy joined Gladys and Tes in their collection of potion ingredients, I glanced around the Quad, taking notice of something off.

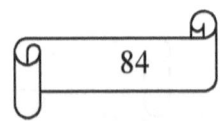

"Where's Valentin?" I asked myself, softly enough so that Guy and the girls couldn't hear over the rain.

I saw his booth and nothing else. Not even Colby was there.

Did something happen? Maybe he went back to Shroudolous... I hope he's okay...

Colby warmed his whiskers next to the blue fire in the cave that he and Valentin decided to reside in for the night.

"So," Valentin kindled the flame with a stray grey branch. "If we go back to Shroudolous, Valaeria will reduce us to dust and if I *don't* go back then I live in this cave and live off of Gryphon meat instead of those weird sausages Corbé had. Either side isn't very ideal, huh?"

Valentin looked to the rat who, once dried, got onto Valentin's lap to curl up for a little nap.

"You don't know a word I'm saying," Valentin sighed. "Kind of figured. Goodnight anyway."

With minimal movements so to not wake up Colby, Valentin got comfortable and closed his eyes to rest.

At this point, you understand my routine to get to my nightly training. The only difference was that I was wearing one of Valentin's hoodies on my sprint to meet Black Silver. My master was standing in the rain and next to a large circular stone.

"'Ello," I said, pulling out my mason jar with Rick inside who was still eating her breakfast, lunch, and dinner. "So, what's in store for today's training?"

"Apprentice Corbé," Black Silver's voice cut through the pouring rain. "thou hath become aware of the three sorts of Light Spectrum abilities, howe'er, we shall delve into the darkness for thine next few lessons."

"Okay," I nodded as I unscrewed Rick's jar. "She's not going to get snuffed out in the rain, is she?"

"Sprites art stronger than one may think," Black Silver said. "She shall survive."

I released Rick from the jar and allowed her to hover. Even though she didn't fizzle out from the water, she did still stick herself in my hood to avoid getting wet.

"What kind of 'darkness' are we delving into?" I asked my master.

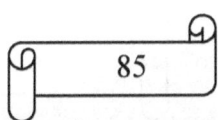

"Thine new ability, Destruction. Thine task for the evening be to destroy this stone before thee. Thou shall use thine Sprite to carry out this task."

I glanced at Rick in my confusion before returning my befuddlement to Black Silver.

"Like how? Do I throw her or something?" I kidded with Rick slapping my cheek which was essentially like a light tap.

"Sprites art unaffected by alike elemental Spells and may channel their essence, redirecting thine energies into themselves," Black Silver explained.

"So, whatever fire Spell I throw at Rick, she'll be able to use it for herself?" I attempted to clarify.

"Verily," Black Silver nodded.

"Ready?" I asked the Sprite.

Rick gave a shrug. She fluttered to the midway point between me and the stone.

"The Spell of Destruction is a craft that requires sight beyond sight," Black Silver said. "Take in thine surroundings, every inch of it. Use all of thine senses to detect everything around thee."

I did as Black Silver instructed. Although the rain made it difficult to see everything, I analysed everything that I could through the water droplets. Once I took in every tree, speck of dirt or puddle of mud, and inch of rock, I shut my eyes. The scent of wet wood and petrichor was fresh to my nose. My skin tingled from the cold of the rain and the heat off of Rick. As I breathed in through my mouth, I could detect the subtle scent and taste of smoke in the air coupled with the residual sweat on my upper lip from my run. Every drop of rain echoed against the environment that all started from far away until reaching us with their light trickles that turned to a torrent of sound waves.

After my prep was complete, I opened my eyes to allow Black Silver to carry on further instruction.

"Destruction requires imagination. Thou must not desire thine target to merely be destroyed. Imagine every inch of thine surroundings and how it shall react once thine target is gone," Black Silver said. "Imagine the rain reaching the dirt beneath the stone without interruption. Imagine the sounds being able to reach thee without hindrance. Imagine a world without thine target in it. If thou art successful, thee shall be able to demolish near any target."

"Like the Behemoth Touch?" I asked, poising my hands to draw the Destruction Spell.

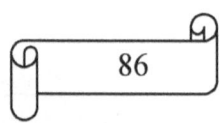

"Nay. The Behemoth Touch be a manoeuvre unparalleled to any. Thine Destruction Spell may demolish many-a-thing in this world, howbeit thee shall not be able to destroy everything."

The Behemoth Touch we were speaking of was basically like a fighting dance routine that once done could destroy any one thing in your path. That or it would destroy *you*. It was absurdly powerful, but I'd only managed to do it once. A Destruction Spell seemed to be a vastly dumbed down version of it with less bodily risk.

"Direct thine Spell to Lady Rick so she may carry out the intended task. Prepared?" Black Silver asked, stepping away from the stone.

"Verily," I smirked with a nod.

I began with the sword in the middle of all Spells before building out the four star-legs that would produce the full spell. Once it was formed, I gave it a right good punch towards Rick who absorbed it like it was nothing. Rick's currently blue fire and skin was illuminated red like my Spell. My Sprite lit on fire with her taking a page from my book and forming her own Spell. Rick sent out her Destruction Spell at the stone which smashed it into chunks which turned to dust and then burned into nonexistent.

"Beautifully done, Apprentice Corbé," Black Silver complimented. "Likewise, Lady Rick."

"Thank you, Master Silver," I bowed to him.

According to Rick, our lesson was done for the day since she retreated into her mason jar to dry off. With a nod in my direction, Black Silver turned to leave as well.

"Oi, Master Silver," I called to the black knight before he could get too far. "Were you going to show up to the Valentine's Day Ball tomorrow?"

"I shall give it some thought," Black Silver spoke over his shoulder on his way to wherever he always went off to.

It'd be nice to see Black Silver enjoy himself. He's actually pretty great at parties.

I faced towards the kingdom of Dolorous with a sort of heaviness settling in my stomach. I couldn't pinpoint why, but I could detect that something was amiss. That threat that Valaeria warned me of seemed more real now. Even though Valentin was gone, I could feel his presence.

I can't see the threat, I thought as I clenched my fist in its cold and wet state. *But that doesn't mean it's not present.*

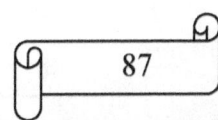

Rudy landed right next to me and shaded me as I stood to gaze upon my kingdom. Without looking, I retrieved mine and Rudy's visors to clasp onto our faces. As I mounted the Questing Beast, I mushed her to take to the air.

There's something not right here… Something's about to change.

"Hey, kid, you doing all right?" A sly and sleazy voice sounded off in the cave with Valentin.

Valentin sat up straight, awaking from his slumber to locate the source of the voice. It was hard to miss the panda sitting in the corner. When Valentin looked to Mickey Vague, he groaned in his throat as he tried to get comfortable again.

"What are you supposed to be?" Valentin moped.

"I'm supposed to be the one to give you the answer to your prayers," Mickey Vague's words piqued Valentin's interest, but he refused to look at him. "I have an offer for you."

"Sorry, but I don't have any money," Valentin huffed, kicking a bone he and Colby cleaned the meat off of for their dinner.

"I don't work for money, kid," Mickey Vague stepped closer to Valentin, looming over him as he reached into a pocket of his hiking pack.

"I'm not a kid," Valentin corrected the panda.

"Compared to me, *everyone* is a kid," The panda said, retrieving the item he was offering to Valentin. "This is for you."

Valentin turned to see the golden flute that was being held by Mickey Vague. It seemed like a normal duct flute except for the purple gemstone that was at its very end.

"What's so special about that thing?" Valentin asked, facing completely towards the sketchy merchant.

"It's not what's special about this thing that's important," Mickey dangled the flute as if it was completely expendable. "It's what's special about *you*."

Mickey tossed the flute to Valentin who snatched it out of the air. Colby got onto Valentin's shoulder and sniffed the flute in the same sort of interest that Valentin was looking at it with. Valentin delicately ran his fingers over the flute.

"Go ahead," Mickey gestured for Valentin to play the instrument.

"I don't know how to play," He said.

"Everyone starts somewhere."

"Well, I… hmm…"

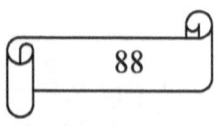

After buffing the mouthpiece with his cape, Valentin rose the flute to his mouth and gave it a single blow. The ear piercingly off-key note filled the cave causing Mickey and Colby's ears to fold over themselves.

"Sorry..." Valentin grimaced. "Umm..."

Valentin inhaled through his nose, poised his mouth again, but this time he breathed his special breath into the fife. As the air passed through the instrument, the purple gemstone glowed brightly. Despite the fact that his fingers didn't move from the holes on the flute, the same note from before was transformed into the most elegant and beautiful sound.

In a possession level trance, Colby dropped off of Valentin's shoulder, sat in front of him, and stared at the flute player in awe. Valentin knit his brows quizzically at Colby's strange behaviour. Valentin swayed himself to the right to find that Colby mimicked him. He did the same for the other side with the same result.

The Fiend rose from the ground and walked backwards with Colby keeping time with his pace. Still playing his flute, Valentin removed one hand from it to poise palm-side up. As if taking a wordless command, Colby crawled up Valentin's body to sit himself in his hand.

The moment that Valentin stopped playing the pipe, Colby shook himself out of his hypnotic state.

"You can do a lot more than just control *one* rat," Mickey Vague told Valentin. "So, kid..." He chuckled as headed for the cave's exit. "what're you going to do with that power of yours?"

Colby and Valentin cast their stares to the golden flute in their possession. A long, daunting, vexatious crisis of conscience battled itself within the Fiend's brain before one side won out.

"Time for this little trip of mine to finally pay off," Valentin looked to Colby.

A mischievous, Fiendish smile drew itself upon Valentin's obscure face.

"Big day, big day, big day," I psyched myself up as I woke up.

After my night training with Black Silver, I decided to stay up for a while and create invites for the ball. I couldn't sleep out of my anticipation. Whether it was for the ball or if it was the looming 'change' that Lancelot foretold, I wasn't sure. It only took a few hours to make the invites from the same sort of cardstock I used to make my

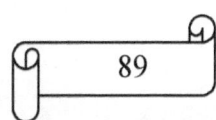

personal playing cards. To fake fanciness, I used a golden marker on the multicoloured cards to write.

'You are cordially invited to Corbé Le Fay's first annual Valentine's Day Ball! Dancing: Required. Night of epic fun: Of course. Follow the Bronze Knights to the Secret Cathedral beneath the royal castle. Party starts at Violet Fire! Your Queen loves you, Dolorous!' Hmm, I smiled to myself. *I've always wanted to use the word 'cordially'.*

Once I was done, I tucked the invites into my knapsack and was about to catch a few winks before my Bluetooth rang.

"Who needs sleep anyway?" I lazily rolled myself off of my bed to get within minimum reaching range of my earpiece on my chest of drawers. "'Ello?"

"Apprentice Corbé," Black Silver spoke over the line.

"Master Silver, calling to RSVP?" I asked.

"Nay. I desire thee to come to thine rendezvous this morning. I would nigh wish to derail thine plans for the evening."

"Yeah, sure," I covered my mouth to suppress a yawn. "That sounds doable, I'm going to have to grab a morning coffee or something but I'll meet you soon."

"Until then, Apprentice Corbé," Black Silver said before hanging up.

After slipping into my workout clothes, I exited my bedroom to be greeted with Raiden leaned against the opposite wall with a warm coffee in hand and an Ever Chill in the other.

"Morning," Raiden smiled to me.

"Morning," I returned the grin. "Were you eavesdropping or something?" I asked as I took the offered quick breakfast.

"No, just got a feeling you'd need it," Raiden shrugged.

"Speaking of feelings…"

I excitedly dipped my Ever Chill into my piping hot coffee so I could nosh down. Ever Chill had the magical property of being remarkably cold which played well with the coffee to form a flavourful steam in my mouth. I lolled my head back as I savoured the flavour combination.

"Thank you. I needed this," I murmured as I enjoyed the sensation with plumes of steam seeping out of the corners of my mouth.

"Looks like. Think of it as a thank you for the Guinebeer yesterday."

"Just another reason to buy more," I giggled. "O, while I have you," I reached into my knapsack and held out my cards. "Could you have someone deliver these? They're invites for tonight."

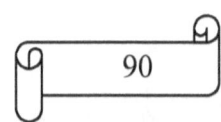

"I could do it for you," Raiden volunteered, taking the deck of cards from me.

"I would love that," I gave my royal adviser a hug. "All right," I hastily finished off my biscuit and drink and gave my mug back to Raiden. "I'll see you tonight. I need to go for an early training sesh with Black Silver."

"Make sure you get some rest when you get back," Raiden urged me.

"Will do."

In my rush to say goodbye and head out, I gave Raiden a kiss on the cheek before leaving.

Uh... Did I just kiss Raiden goodbye? I asked myself. *Let's just pretend I didn't and move on.*

Out of my determination to leave the castle as quickly as possible, I ran with no intention of stopping until I met with Black Silver.

In the Quad, the man in Inuit sunglasses waited around the corner of a fruit stand. The merchant who had just made a transaction tucked their Phlorin into a money box under the booth's counter. Before it shut, the thief snagged a fistful of Phlorin from the box, shoved it into his pocket, and slipped away before the merchant noticed.

"Haha," The man patted his pocket with a laugh. "Merchant Week gets better and easier every year."

As he walked off with his morning 'earnings', a sound petrified him in place. A majestic melody entranced the thief to face towards the source of the music. Down the road was Valentin playing his golden pipe. Once under his spell, the thief had no choice but to come closer and empty his pockets in front of the Fiend. Hundreds of Phlorin decorated the road in front of them.

Colby dropped from Valentin's shoulder with a size changing drawstring bag to collect their reward.

After Colby returned to Valentin's shoulder, the new musician walked down the street towards a sewer grate that he'd opened earlier. Valentin stepped over the hole to lure the thief to drop into the Dolorean sewer. The Fiend kicked the lid back into place with only his leg strength alone. With the thief dealt with, Colby squeaked happily in victory.

Valentin was about to leave the area, but he decided to inspect what other contents of the thief's pockets were there. There were a few paperclips, a rubber band, and a playing card that was written on in

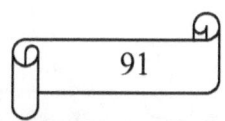

golden script. Valentin read the invite to the Valentine's Day Ball with a sombre frown.

"Corbé…" Valentin and Colby exchanged guilty looks. "What would she think? Maybe we should-"

"Are you going to the ball tonight?" A familiar voice to Valentin came from the Quad.

At the fruit stand was the woman who haggled Valentin down to five Phlorin the other day. She was speaking to a friend of hers as they picked out their fruits.

"Of course, I'm going. Corbé's bound to throw one Hell of a party."

"They don't call her the Rockstar of Dolorous for nothing," The haggler laughed.

"Did you figure out what you're going to wear?"

"Yes, I bought the cutest sweater the other day. I got it so cheap too."

"How cheap?" Her friend asked.

"Just five."

"No way! You've got to show me it!"

Valentin grinded his teeth in anger as he backed away from the pair of women. With his fingers clenching around his golden pipe, Valentin walked off to collect his thoughts.

"Colby, we need to make more bags," Valentin looked over the invite one more time before tucking the card into his tunic pocket. "because we're just getting started."

One of the only perks to ageing faster than a sliced open avocado was the fact that I had a surplus of energy on hand despite my initial groggy state. That being in mind, I was able to arrive at Black Silver's lesson just as orange fire was starting.

"Good morning, Master Silver," I greeted the knight. "Hmm, feels like it's been forever since I've said that. You're not really a morning person, are you?"

"'Tis narrowly in mine preference, aye," Black Silver gave a half-shrug.

"So, what's today's lesson?" I asked as Rudy crashed down nearby with a Dive-Bomb.

"Today thou shall learn to conduct Manipulation."

"Manipulation," I repeated out of mere reflex.

"Thee may raise and snuff out a flame that be not thine, howe'er, this power extends further than mere elements. The mind may likewise

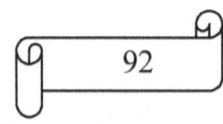

be affected. Confidence be the most important aspect of this Spell Craft. Thou must place thine emotions above someone else's. Thine thoughts and feelings must overwhelm and overshadow thine target's. One must believe that thine existence be more important than the other's."

"That… That sounds super creepy," I took a half step away from my master.

"The power of Dark Magic be strong yet one must relinquish thine attachments to execute. Those of whom art emotionally distant to many may overshadow others more simply, their conscience be muddled and obscured. Destruction, Manipulation, and Death art the most devastating of Witch Craft and art likely to damage thine enemy or thee. Thine fire Spell may overshadow fire and fire based beings. If thine Spell be strong enough, thee can overshadow near anyone regardless of element. Thou shall conduct thine matter of Manipulation upon thine Sprite."

I'm going to mind control Rick? I looked at the nonchalant Sprite in the mason jar.

"Master Silver, I…"

"Apprentice Corbé, thou must trust me as I hath placed mine trust in thee," Black Silver asserted. "'Tis merely meant for thine educational purposes. Thine Sprite shall not feel a thing."

"O-okay… Master Silver," I exhaled a breath to steel my nerves.

After releasing Rick and having her hover in front of me, we faced each other so I could conduct my Spell.

My needs are more important than yours, I tried to tell myself with a large amount of doubt.

"Draw thine Spell," Black Silver ordered.

Regardless of my reluctance to conduct the Spell, I carved the peculiar shape. It started with a plus sign and then had diagonals coming out of the points. According to archives I'd read, it was supposed to symbolise a marionette controller.

My needs are above yours, I stared into Rick's eyes which perpetually softened my intense mindset.

"Focus on what thou want thine target to conduct," Black Silver said.

I am stronger than you, I lied to myself, poising my hand in front to send out my Spell.

"Cast thine Spell," Black Silver said harshly.

My existence is…

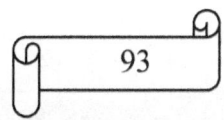

Even before I could finish the thought, my mind flickered. Seeing the Sprite in her orange state and holding such an understanding gaze made me remember the only woman I came close to calling my mother. Rick reminded me of my protector… my guardian… the Lady of the Lava…

Lotl… My hand retracted from the Spell. *I can't do it.*

"Apprentice Corbé," Black Silver folded his arms. "Conduct thine Spell."

"I can't," I mumbled.

"Speak up," Black Silver commanded.

"I can't!" I barked at my master. "Rick's a wanker and an ingrate, but I'm not going to mind control her. It doesn't feel right," I held my forearms as I cheated myself away from Black Silver.

"Do thine Spell," Black Silver brought his arms to his sides as he clenched his fists.

"No!"

"Thine Master hast given thou an order!"

"And I said no!" I faced Black Silver while stamping a foot.

"Perhaps thou art too immature to carryout thine lessons," Black Silver sighed. "After all, thee art merely a child unfit for thine family's throne."

"Excuse me?" I squinted at the black knight.

"Thou art an impetuous child and thine parents would undoubtedly be displeased with thee," Black Silver stroked Cath sombrely.

"Shut up," I tensed my jaw.

"Perhaps Dolorous be not the home as thee had first thought. Thou belong back in thine mortal Terrace home," Black Silver said with disappointment.

"I said for you to shut up," I spoke behind grinding my teeth.

"Speak thine words clearly, Apprentice Corbé!" Black Silver shouted.

"I said SHUT UP!" I ferally roared.

The Spell that still hovered in front of Rick travelled along my voice's shockwave, blew past the Sprite, and slammed directly into Black Silver's chest. The black knight crippled to his knees as an overwhelming red aura encompassed him. Before I could go all Wicked on him, I snapped out of my momentary rage.

"Shit," I gasped. "I-I'm sorry… I…"

Black Silver progressively rose from the dirt with a black energy taking over the subsiding red.

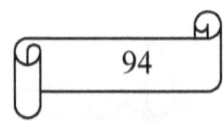

"I'm sorry, Master Silver," I inched away from the fast approaching knight. "I didn't mean to. I-I…"

Before I could react, Black Silver held my shoulder, pulled me towards himself and embraced me. Although his armour was cold and he was overly strong, the gesture was warm and delicate.

"I did not mean mine words, Apprentice Corbé," Black Silver assured me as I returned the hug. "I knew how thee would react… and what thee would do. Thou art right for thine throne and thee make thine parents proud wherever they art every day."

Once Black Silver released me, he gently placed a hand on my neck with his thumb rubbing my cheek.

"Thine lesson for today be over," Black Silver spoke softly.

His sterling eyes were filled with pride and kindness which confirmed his emotional parenthetical.

"You're such an arse," I giggled with my eyes nearly brimming with tears of either belated anger or spontaneous elation.

"Likewise to thee, Apprentice Corbé," Black Silver laughed.

Rick fluttered up to me. Her face didn't really emote much so it was hard to tell what she was thinking.

Can Sprites talk? I asked myself.

Regardless, wordlessly, Rick gave me a light punch on the cheek with only the slightest curl of the corner of her mouth.

I'll take that as a, 'Thanks for not mind controlling me'.

"You're welcome," I whispered to Rick.

The Sprite sat herself on my shoulder instead of going back into her jar so she could lean on my neck.

"Well, I guess I'll be heading out," I said to Black Silver, stashing my empty mason jar into Rudy's side-satchel.

"If it be all the same with thee, Apprentice Corbé," Black Silver placed a hand on Rudy's hide. "I wish to walk thee to thine castle today."

Rudy looked to me and gave a relaxed shrug.

"I think that'd be great," I smiled.

Once Black Silver and I started on our way back to town, Rudy and Cath both headed their separate ways.

"I hope thou knowest that I would ne'er speak of thee so lowly with a serious mind, mine Apprentice," Black Silver told me.

"That's good to know," I said.

"Art there any matters that trial thine mind that thou wish to speak of?" Black Silver tried to make conversation.

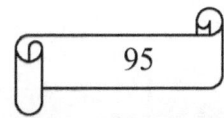

"Only one thing."

"What matter?"

"Are you going to the ball?"

With a laugh filled sigh, Black Silver ruffled my hair as we continued our walk.

"Seriously though."

Valentin crashed in a kneeling position down one of the manholes of the Dolorean sewer system. On his back, he carried a sling bag filled with the same kind of sacks that he used to steal back his money. The Fiend surveyed the tunnels for any walks of life, but none were visible to him.

"This is the spot?" Valentin asked Colby who squeaked positively. "I trust you."

With a deep inhale, Valentin poised the lip plate into place and gave a hearty blow through the flute. A wickedly melodious wind let loose throughout the sewer that reached every crack, crevice, and hole beneath Dolorous.

As the same song as before played itself out, the rhythmic footfalls of vermin accompanied the flute's notes. Leagues of rats filled the tunnel where Valentin and Colby were, taking up the floor like a sentient shag carpet.

The rodents clustered around Valentin's ankles and looked to him, awaiting his command even after he had lowered the golden flute from his lips.

"She did say that she was expecting us at her ball tonight," Valentin justified solemnly, petting Colby relaxingly. "She's just going to get a little more than she bargained for."

Valentin waded through the rodents, dropping his bag in the centre of the furry mass.

"Everyone take one," Valentin said, poising his flute back up to his lips. "and follow me."

The rats did as commanded, trailing on Valentin's heels as he led the way towards the royal palace.

More of the same. I went to town, did my rounds of the booths, and headed to make sure the ball preparations were complete. I was elated to see that everyone in Dolorous had their invites and were now rushing around to prepare for the ball.

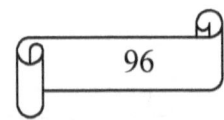

Although I was excited for the evening's festivities, I was disheartened by the fact that neither Valentin nor Colby were in the Quad. A part of me was expecting him to reappear any second now, but no such luck. My perception of his skills and workmanship in tailoring overshadowed my idea of his possible danger to my kingdom.

But still… I unglued my eyes from Valentin's empty booth so I could focus on the path ahead of me… *I bet Valentin is a great dancer. I hope Colby's taking care of him, I know my best friend would,* I thought to myself.

I glanced over my shoulder to the far-off birdhouse that Rudy resided in. Her overbearing gaze was constantly fixed on me wherever in the kingdom I went without her. She always watched my back no matter what.

Is it too much to hope that Colby will do the same for Valentin?

As much as I wanted to dwell on the potential fate of the missing Fiend, I still had an entire Kingdom to take care of.

When I entered my bedroom, I found a Valentin brand violet one-shoulder flower stitch dress, a pair of black flats, nude leggings, my scarf, my beret, my friendship bracelet, and my cape with a note on top of the laid-out wardrobe. Rick was sitting right next to the outfit, smirking from obviously already reading the note for herself.

I bit my lip as I read, *'Thought you'd like this outfit. Can't wait for tonight ^-^ – Rai'.*

"That boy," I smiled as I gathered the clothes and headed to the bathroom. "I think I'm liking this new Raiden."

I washed up and slipped into Raiden's preferred outfit, doing a twirl in the mirror.

"So, Rick," I faced the Sprite when I reentered my bedroom. "How's this outfit?"

Rick gave a smile coupled with a shrug.

"Well, that's better than before," I murmured to myself. "You're coming to the ball, right?"

My question filled the tiny Sprite with discomfort, her rubbing the back of her neck with a less playful shrug.

"You don't dance?" I asked. "Fine, I'll just let you hang out with Rudy for the night."

Rick fluttered up to me and gave me a light punch on my cheek before gathering her things to have her sleepover at Rudy's. Her

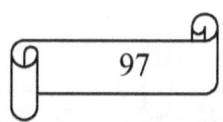

'things' consisted of her jar, a tiny vile of nectar I'd purchased for her, and a sugarplum of course.

Once I was alone, I took the opportunity to check my outfit one more time. Modestly speaking, I looked great and I was elated to know that Raiden felt the same way. Since I already knew what Raiden would be wearing for the night, my mind went away with itself imaging the two of us dancing all night in the Secret Cathedral.

A knock on the door snapped me out of my romantic dream state.

"Coming," I informed my visitor. "Probably the man of the hour himself," I smiled to myself.

Upon opening my door, I instinctively backed up and produced my aura shield and sword in my battle-ready stance. Tes threw her arms up in half-innocence and half-shock.

"I come in peace," Tes hastily informed.

The court jester carried no weapons, not even her usual lute, showing that she was ball-ready. Tes wore a long-sleeved indigo bodycon dress with slits down the sides of her torso. Something I couldn't help but notice was that Tes had several tattoos on her body that seemed to be serpentine, covered in feathers, or other animalistic designs which were too obstructed to make out anything in specific.

I allowed myself to lower my guard and soon after my aura armaments dissolved into silver dust.

"Sorry, Tes," I said, exiting the bedroom to lock my door and join her in the hall. "I've been on edge all day."

"And here I thought it was because you didn't trust me."

"Eh," I gave a fifty-fifty gesture. "Column A, Column B."

"Why're you on edge? I didn't take you for the type to be nervous over a dance," Tes asked.

Moving our conversation down the hall, I tried to clear my mind and put my thoughts into words.

"Lancelot told me something that I'm worried about," I said.

"How is he?" Tes asked with poorly subdued urgency.

"He's taking incarceration fairly well. His insanity passed the first week and now he just spends his time spouting out pearls of wisdom."

"So... why do you still have him locked up?"

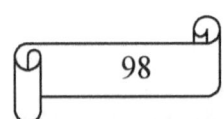

"Tes, you know precisely why I still have him locked up," I folded my arms to prevent me from reanimating my aura armaments. "The real question you should be asking is why don't I have *you* locked up."

"My apologies," Tes gave me some space as we continued down the passage towards the stairs. "I just really wish that Lancelot would be free right now. That sash of yours…" The jester's eyes narrowed on the scarf around my neck. "That thing corrupts people or rather it *did* until you cured Dolorous. That's all I'm saying. It might not've been Lancelot making those decisions."

"Possibly, but I still need to make sure that that's the case before I allow him anywhere near any diamond spitting creatures or razor-sharp weapons."

"I understand," Tes begrudgingly nodded. "Going back to the 'pearl of wisdom' Lancelot gave you, what was it?"

"Right," Thinking back to it almost made me stumble down the steps, but I caught myself on the railing. "Lancelot said that rain symbolises change. It rained shortly after King Arthur died, it rained when I took to being chancellor of Dolorous, and it rained this week. It makes me worry that there's something coming soon that I might not be prepared for."

"Corbé, if there's anything that I've learned from watching you do your thing it's that there is nothing that you're not prepared for," Tes said.

"In the one instance," I grumpily added.

"I honestly don't care what you think of yourself, I've been around for aeons and I know when someone's aura is fabulous when I see it," Tes assured me.

"Golly gee willikers, thanks, Tes," I said with possibly more than a hint of sarcasm.

Fabulousness wasn't really a quantifiable essence in my mind, but I understood the jester's sentiment.

The deeper into the castle we went, the more audible the sound of clicking heels, rattling jewellry, and chattering mouths became. Tes and I slowed our steps once we saw the impenetrable wall of Doloreans all funnelling into the narrow passage towards the Secret Cathedral.

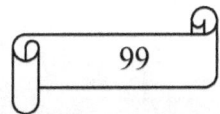

"Woof," I scratched my heel with my toes. "I never thought that I would have to wait to get into my own party."

"You're kidding, right?" Tes asked me.

"What do you mean?"

"Ahem," Tes cleared her throat. "Hear ye! Hear ye!" The jester barked across the crowd of commoners. "Make way for your princess!"

Without any semblance of hesitation, every Dolorean parted way on either side to allow me access to the Secret Cathedral hall. As I passed by everyone, they graciously bowed their heads to me. Even though I thought I made it pretty clear that I wasn't really into the whole 'formal greeting thing' they still lowered their heads to me.

Eh, maybe they'll soon understand the artform of the 'crowd running high five'.

I sauntered down the steps until passing through the now covered up hall of statues. They were masked beneath veils of shrubbery so they looked more like hedges and not grave watchers. Beyond the golden gates, I found commoners mingling, eating off of the floating hors d'oeuvre trays, and sipping champagne.

The main event hadn't started yet since the band wasn't ready. Something that disheartened me was that Guy and his band were setting up without a Snapback in sight. What with our talk earlier, I wasn't surprised that the little Burrowing Eagle didn't want to come. Although I understood, that didn't make me feel better about it.

"'Ello, maestro," I approached Guy, placing my elbow on the stage as I leaned towards him. "How's tricks?"

Guy greeted me and explained his excitement about his set for the night and the new equipment that they had obtained. Although I was listening to him, I couldn't help but notice a cold chill snaking throughout the entire cathedral. It wasn't a normal draught, it was one with ominous connotations.

"Ah, and Corbé," Guy rounded off to a different topic other than his music set. "The potion will be ready within an hour."

Guy gestured to an ancient cauldron on the beverage table made out of eroded black stone and silvery steel that was labelled 'Το Δοχείο Αναζωογόνησης'. For those of you who are thinking 'It's all Greek to me', you'd actually be correct because it *is* Greek. It roughly translated

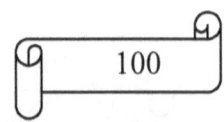

to 'The Revitalising Container' or 'The Cauldron of Rejuvenation'. I think I read something in the Lightitome about it, but I couldn't pinpoint its importance. The only thing that was important to me was that it held my anti-ageing potion.

I would've pointed out to Guy that that was a bad place to put it, in front of everyone next to the punch bowl, but it was apparent to everyone that they should avoid it. They were even doing their best to keep their distance by getting their punch at arm's reach.

"Can't wait," I perked from seeing the cauldron brewing itself to a boil. "At least that's one less thing that I have to stress my hair white over."

"How horrible that must be," Guy said in monotone.

"Yeah, I said it," I folded my arms, standing firm on my statement. "Have you ever had a gut feeling that something bad was coming?"

"In my line of work, that becomes a part of the job," Guy said. "What's the feeling today?"

"I don't know, something's coming, I can tell, but I don't know when," I looked over the room as if one of the people attending the festivity was my latest enemy in disguise.

"Here, I was saving this for you," Guy said, producing two champagne glasses from just off stage. "It might help."

"It sounds nice right about now," I took the glass he offered and toasted. "It *is* a party after all."

We swigged our champagne down with satisfied smacks and set them down on stage.

"I really needed that," I groaned.

"Shall we get this party started?" Guy offered me his microphone.

"We shall," I joined the band on stage, tapping the microphone to grab the Doloreans' attention. "Good evening, Dolorous, how's everyone doing tonight?!" I sang.

The tipsy commoners whooped and hollered, raising their glasses to me.

"That's what I like to hear! We're starting this shindig, so grab your partner and drop your glasses!"

Everyone in the Secret Cathedral placed their drinks down on the floating trays so that they could hit the dance floor as Guy took to his

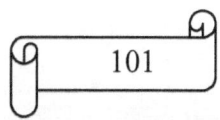

guitar. With the music cuing up, the Doloreans took to the upbeat sock-hop style song.

I did quick vocal warmups before taking the microphone and letting loose to the song.

'Kick off your shoes, you're in for a treat.
Wake up your neighbours right down the street.
I got a song with the rhythm and beat,
that's gonna make you wanna move your feet.
It's that new school sound, that 50s tune,
gonna send you BANG! ZOOM! Straight to the moon!
It goes ooh-pang-bang, pow-pow-pow.
Zing-zang-zop, me-meow.
Zip-zap flop, la-la-loon,
gonna send you...?'

"BANG! ZOOM! Straight to the moon!" The Doloreans finished up the lyrics for me as they rocked out.

For the ones who didn't know how to dance to the music, I led the crowd from the stage with fancy footwork and hip sways. Eventually, the Doloreans did me proud and took to the dance moves so that I could take five and take in the room. From my position, I could see all of the modifications that Raiden had added to the Cathedral, me noting the latest being the net of balloons on the ceiling.

Nice touch, Aderyn, I mentally complimented.

Shifting my gaze to the guests, I spotted Tes dancing with Gladys near the beverage table. I never expected to see them palling around together, but I suppose Tes was full of surprises.

Speaking of surprises, it looked like someone had one of their own. Among the latecomers to the party was one who was garbed in a full suit of black armour.

"My o' my," I gawked at the sight of my master. "Guy, take over for me."

I handed Guy's microphone back to him so I could join the crowd.

Black Silver gravitated towards one of the seats, but he wasn't able to sit down since I snagged him by his elbow spike and pulled him onto the dance floor.

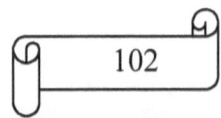

"Ever heard this song before?!" I asked above the ruckus of the party, dancing all the while.

"Aye, one time before," Black Silver nodded.

"Do you know how to dance?!"

"A good Master must be a Master of all crafts," Black Silver said.

"So… you dance?!"

With the steely light of his eyes lightening and a slight chuckle, Black Silver took my hand and danced flawlessly to the music which earned an uncontrollable laughing fit from me.

Master of all crafts, including sock-hop! Greatest. Master. Ever!

Guy continued the song, "It goes ooh-pang-bang, pow-pow-pow. Zing-zang-zop, me-meow. Zip-zap-flop, la-la-loon. Gonna send you…?"

"BANG! ZOOM! Straight to the moon!" Black Silver and I shouted together louder than anyone else in the Cathedral.

Although the moment was unbelievably fantastic, there was a looming worry in my mind. A worry that superseded everything else at the moment…

Where the heck is my date?!

Thirty minutes earlier…

Raiden Aderyn was leaning off the edge of one of the balconies, tethering a large net of confetti to the ceiling behind an enormous amount of red, blue, green, white, black, gold, silver, and purple helium balloons. Below, Guy, Tes, and Gladys were brewing my anti-ageing potion at the beverage table, keeping an eye on the Aderyn son as he worked.

"Gladys, does your kid have something against ladders? I've never seen the little bastard sword use one," Guy asked the Aderyn mother.

"Come to think of it…" Gladys pondered that for a moment.

"You're gonna break your neck, kid!" Tes hollered up to Raiden as she added a handful of herbs to The Cauldron of Rejuvenation.

"Thank you for your votes of confidence," Raiden sarcastically said with a chuckle subtext.

"Speaking of confidence, I can't believe that you actually managed to ask Corbé to the ball," Gladys perked. "Good on you."

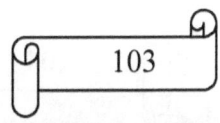

"Thanks, mum, doubly for the advice," Raiden said.

"Well then, extra parent points for me," Gladys smiled to herself satisfactorily.

The comment drew a topic to Guy's attention which he seemed reluctant to bring up.

"Gladys," Guy said cautiously.

"Mhm?" Gladys hummed.

"I don't mean to be a noodge-"

"You're always a noodge," Tes butted in.

"Only when I'm working," Guy sassed. "Anyway," He redirected his attention to Gladys. "I was curious on something…"

"Use your words, Guy," Gladys advised.

"Is Drake's mission going well?"

Gladys' stirring slowed and her face fell at the same progressive pace as if the Aderyn mother had never known how to smile. She was blank and thoughtless and stared vacantly into the brew that the three of them were making. Tes' expression sunk into the same sort of stupor that Gladys was going through. The merchant stared up at the Aderyn son overhead who had stopped working to become motionless.

"I'm sorry, I didn't-"

Guy was halted midsentence to become hypnotised by the faintest of musical notes, the same song that took hold of Gladys, Tes, and Raiden.

Gladys raised her head for a moment, only to lower it down as if she nodded off into sleep. Tes did likewise which was then followed by Guy doing the same. However, when Raiden raised his head, his irises dilated like that of a serpent's.

Raiden's body glowed orange and red which produced two flame-like creatures over his shoulders. The first was a ram and the second was a dragon. The two of them swirled together in a dancing fashion until merging into a yin-yang symbol of the two beasts.

Raiden allowed himself to fall backwards off of the balcony. Instead of splatting onto the golden floor, he landed in a kneeling position with no sign of damage or injury.

The Aderyn child's movements were that of a wind-up soldier, marching mindlessly, robotically, and relentlessly to the beat of music that grew more pronounced the further down the hall Raiden went. His

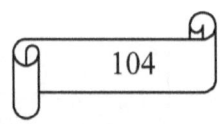

face was as lifeless as the stone statues that he passed by on his way to the wall just next to the spiral staircase. It seemed to be a simple petrified mass of ashen grey stone, but something of note was that there was a subtle protrusion in its centre.

As Raiden placed his hand on the mound on the wall, a similar effect as before was produced from Raiden, his body sending out two flames. The red fire remained the same, a dragon, but the new one was a black bat form which fused together with the red one before flickering away.

Beyond the millennia old layers of dust and rust on the wall Raiden was touching, a large keyhole was revealed. Under Raiden's fingers, the tumblers inside the wall grinded together until coming to a clicking halt.

The wall retracted like a sliding door to reveal the pied piper himself, Valentin, at the forefront of an enormous mischief of rats. He lowered the golden flute from his mouth to address his temporary mind puppet.

"Danke, Raiden, you've been kind to me," Valentin placed a gentle hand on his shoulder. "I don't want you here for tonight. Go home and stay there for one-to-two hours or so. When that's done, you come here and show Corbé a good time, eh?" Before Valentin resealed the passage, he added hastily. "O and also, forget you ever saw me here, ja? You three too!" He pointed to Guy, Gladys, and Tes down the way.

"Yes, sir," All four of them responded.

Once Valentin closed the wall, leaving it ajar, Raiden continued his zombie walk up the stairs and back to the Aderyn household. Gladys, Guy, and Tes all resumed from their mental time freeze.

"Drake hasn't kept in contact, but I trust that the mission is going well."

"Drake'll be fine, I'm sure," Tes reassured Gladys. "Aderyns are notorious for being tough cookies."

"Amen," Gladys nodded with a laugh.

"Speaking of which, where's Raiden?"

"He's probably getting more balloons," Guy said.

"He's trying too hard."

"Kind of like someone else I know," Guy murmured under his breath.

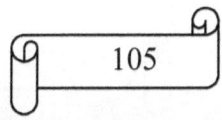

Tes wanted to say something in retaliation, but she bit her tongue just to prove him wrong.

Although Guy and Tes seemed to be at ease about the absence of Raiden, Gladys clearly had a sneaking suspicion that something was wrong.

Back to the party...

Black Silver, master of the sock-hop, breathed heavily as he took a seat with a cup of punch to cleanse his parched throat. As for me, I was still up and kicking since I had so much energy.

In addition to my excitement about the ball, I was eager to hit the drinks table. It had nearly been an hour so that meant that I could partake in Guy's anti-ageing potion.

I'm so ready to be over this whole accelerated ageing thing.

"All righty then," Guy interrupted the current song to make an announcement. "Ladies and gentlemen, we have one more song until we slow things down for a while. So, I hope you've got your dates ready to waltz. Happy Valentine's Day, Dolorous, we love you," He winked and blew a kiss to the crowd.

"I love you!" A random fangirl screamed.

Guy gripped his microphone to cue up the band's next song, but he only got a single inhale in before falling silent. His arm hung limply with his microphone tightly clenched in his grasp and his face contorting into a dumbfounded gawk. One by one, each of Guy's band members did the same, their instruments ringing out their sound until falling silent and being replaced with only one song that carried throughout the entire cathedral. One that was not a part of their music set for the night. It was the sound of a flute. The Doloreans who were in mid-dance all slumped in their postures and dropped their jaws, facing forward like a legion of well-dressed zombies.

I was about to ask Black Silver what was going on, but the same mass trance took hold of my master as well.

"What the He...?"

I could feel my eyes dilate, the music swirling around and through me to lock my joints in place and face me towards the stage like everyone else.

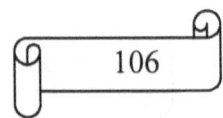

"Everyone! Line up!" The unmistakably distorted German voice yelled from the entrance of the Secret Cathedral.

Like everyone was choreographed ahead of time, all the Doloreans meshed into one massive conga line.

The clicking of heels on the waxed floor resonated loudly, making their way down the line and heading for the right side to gain access to the balconies. Behind the colourful merchant came a mischief of rats that followed closely on his buffed heels. Each rodent held a sack in their mouth which they carried up to the top floor of the cathedral. Once every rat was lined up and held their bags out in front of themselves, Valentin stepped up to the balcony.

Valentin...

Valentin raised his flute to his mouth to resume playing, but something halted him for a moment. Even though I wasn't able to move out of place, my eyes were still able to move about. In that moment of hesitation, Valentin and I had made direct eye contact despite the vast distance that separated us.

With a feral sort of growl, Valentin shut his eyes so he could play uninterrupted. The notes from the flute caused all of us to stand erect, marching forward and up the stairs. Once we were on the move, Valentin flourished his flute to his side.

"I'm going to make this as simple as possible," The Fiend projected. "All of you will drop your valuables into these bags," He gestured to the sacks held by his mind-controlled mice. "Once done, you will leave and forget..." Valentin paused momentarily, sighed, and forced himself to proceed with his instructions. "... and forget you ever saw me... Hop to it!"

Ladies unhooked their pearls, men unclipped their cufflinks, and kids poured their allowances into the seemingly endless grouping of Valentin brand bags. Guy relinquished his microphone, a tonne of Phlorin, and guitar and Gladys tossed in a gold bangle and her clutch purse. The line eventually folded back on itself to lead us towards the doors that led out of the Cathedral, but it would take some time considering we were moving the length of one person every thirty seconds or so. Taking things optimistically, it gave me a lot of time to think.

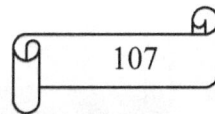

Valentin... I looked up at the Fiend overseeing us on our slow slog to toss away our possessions. *I know why you're doing this, I know that the world's treated you terribly, but I also know one other thing...* Even against my song induced stupor, I clenched my fists until my knuckles popped. *I have to stop you.*

All thought, no bite, right? My mind was racing to come up with a plan to take the Fiend down. Currently, I was outnumbered and from the looks of it, he had both vermin and Doloreans on his side. Whatever my plan was, it would have to be careful, precise, and backed up with *boatloads* of fire power.

Huh... fire power.

A series of thoughts and memories strung themselves together until I found it suitable to call it a plan. It involved *a lot* of destruction, *a lot* of Spell-Casting, and a little bit of wishful thinking. However, the first step was to break free of Valentin's hypnosis.

As the line to surrender our belongings shortened on the rise to the balconies, I tested if I could move my fingers. The entire plan hinged on my ability to do this one little thing. I could ball my fists, so that was a good sign that I had *some* degree of movement in my system despite Valentin's entrancing tune.

You've beaten Lancelot in a flocking Gryphon Joust, you can do this, Corbé.

My fingers unfurled against the force of what seemed like two industrial electromagnets bound together. All of the nerves in my arm went into a full-on tremble to shock my digits back into place, but I fought against it to just get at least one of my fingers out. I allowed my remaining fingers to give up once my index finger was in place.

Blimey, I griped, feeling a bead of sweat coating my brow.

I carefully traced out a one-inch line with my finger. From that line, I drew an 'X' in its centre and a line through it as well. The last step was to curve them together.

What is mind control other than just manipulation of the mind? I asked myself as I finished up my Spell. *And if my lessons have reaped any rewards, then...* I glanced down at the glowing red leaf that hovered in front of my finger. *This should get the job done.*

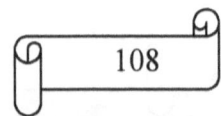

The hovering Spell was just a centimetre out of reach. Thankfully, I was able to uncurl my fingers one more time. I flicked the edge of the Spell with my middle finger which only moved it a bit horizontally.

Come on, I griped.

I grazed the Spell again with the same result.

With feeling this time!

One final flick sent the Spell comfortably into my palm. Allowing Valentin's song to take over again sent my fingers back into fist-form to smash the Spell into vermillion dust in my hand.

A rush of heat travelled all throughout my body, relieving me of the hypnotic trance.

"It worked!" I blurted, immediately covering my mouth.

Glancing upstairs, I found that Valentin was too busy conducting everyone to notice my accidental slip of the tongue.

Next step, I have to get up there.

There was something of interest that I needed from one of the rats' bags. It would take a while for me to reach the top of the stairs, but the art of surprise was always something that Black Silver emphasised in my training.

Once a woman in one of Valentin's sweaters emptied her pockets, the Fiend stopped the line and held her by the shoulder.

"When you leave," He whispered into the woman's ear. "why don't you hike all the way up Wanderer's Peak and jump off, eh?" Valentin chuckled, patting her on her back and bidding her farewell as she headed to leave the cathedral. "Keep it going," Valentin ordered everyone else before starting to play again.

I wondered what the holdup was but, regardless, I had to stay focused.

After the DVLA line of robberies was halfway done, I was finally at the front. Before Valentin spotted me, I allowed my stare to go vacant so he'd believe that I was still under his control.

Valentin removed the fife from his lips and looked at me with a half-frown.

"Corbé, I'm sorry," Valentin sombrely spoke. "I... I gave them a chance... but no one gave *me* one... I like your outfit by the way..."

Val, I internally sighed. *I get it, but this is* my *kingdom and I'm going to defend it... even from a friend.*

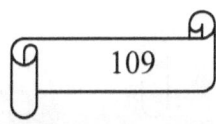

As I passed by the several rows of rats, I spotted the item I needed. The second that my hand brushed by Guy's microphone, I gripped it and leapt off of the balcony. I hooked it around one of the tied-off curtains and pressed my feet into its centre folds to soften my speedy descent down to the ground floor. My actions didn't go unnoticed, however, which I kind of expected.

Valentin flung himself to the balcony to see me sprinting for the entrance to the Secret Cathedral.

"Corbé," Valentin lightly groaned before playing a quick tune on his flute. "Someone," He hollered down to the Doloreans below. "Stop Corbé!"

The closest Doloreans to me all left their positions in line to try to grab at me. From my freehand, I hastily drew out a Spell-Shield. On my run to the massive golden double doors, I used my shield to bash my pursuers away from me. In a scene reminiscent to a zombie apocalypse, the Doloreans rushed for me in a solid wall of grabby hands and slack jawed faces. I did my best to direct my shield to block the zombified Doloreans. Shoving the mass of flesh to one side only opened the other side to be vulnerable.

As fast as I possibly could, I shifted my barrier from left to right until it started to blur between the two positions. Soon enough, the shield had morphed into a much wider barricade that was protecting my hindquarters.

Well, that's nifty. Black Silver's going to have one of his 'Yay, I'm happy that you discovered a new ability, but quit skipping ahead in your studies' talks with me again, isn't he?

I did a 180 and ran backwards so I could give my Aura Barrier a right-good shove to send the wall of Doloreans back a fair distance.

After shoving the doors to the Secret Cathedral open, I took in a huge breath before bellowing into Guy's microphone, "RUDY!"

My shout echoed throughout the castle until I could hear a faint *sukaww!*

Yes, the cavalry's coming, I beamed. *But can't just stand around.*

Without losing any time, I got on my tiptoes to etch out Aura Shields beneath my feet. Stomping into their centres locked them into place at the soles of my slippers.

I leapt over the oncoming mob so I could run across the surface of them as if they were a solid mass.

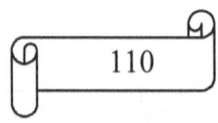

Valentin was taking his time on his descent to my level. He played a quick melody on his flute before pointing to one section of the Doloreans and directing them to me.

The Doloreans that got the order from Valentin leapt up like they were ravenous beasts hungry for a meal. Now serving, Corbé over glass.

"Corbé, please, just let me do this one thing and I'll go," Valentin pleaded with me. "You won't even remember what happened or what I did. You won't even remember *me*. Just let me go."

"I can't let you do that, Val!" I shouted, dodging left and right to avoid the bounding Doloreans. "Not so long as I can stop it!"

I leapt from my position to the beverage table, my Aura Shields shattering from the landing. The Doloreans rushed for me. Quickly, I dropped Guy's microphone so I could draw out several Aura Shields to launch at the commoners. They were large enough for each shield to blast back three or so Doloreans at a time. Although it kept my foes at bay, I was going to eventually run out of steam.

The newfound piper who stood on the stairs almost raised his flute to play again, but lowered it with a groan.

"Corbé!" Valentin bashed his fist into the bannister. "Just give up, I don't want to end up hurting you."

"That's cute how you think you can hurt me," I angled for a cocky tone to rival my disconcerting situation.

Sadly, even though they were brainwashed, they were still the same Doloreans. They learned quickly and they were catching onto my movements.

I need to mix things up a bit... I glanced over to what was next to me and mentally sighed. *It'll work... I guess I'll just have to get Guy to make me that walker.*

I eased up on my bombardment of Shield Spells to conduct a low foot sweep, knocking the Cauldron of Rejuvenation off of the table and spewing a huge outpouring of scarlet liquid to trip up all of the Doloreans around me. They slipped and slid on the blood-like potion, falling over each other or onto their bums.

"For the love of..." Valentin facepalmed with one hand and poised his flute with the other, playing a single note. "Someone! ANYONE! Get her!"

The rest of the line of Doloreans trekked over the slime covered commoners to reach out for me. They still had trouble getting to me which allowed a momentary breather on my part. Just as I was about to

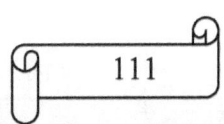

cast out more Spells, the entire cathedral riled up with a pounding, echoing, *SUKAWWW!*

"There's my girl," I grinned.

Rudy dove down the stairs and burst through the doors with such speed that it sent both doors flying off of their hinges. I was prepared to shield the Doloreans from the incoming monoliths of gold, but Rudy was already on it. The Questing Beast swung her backside around so she would slide on the potion covered floor on her bum.

As Rudy was coming in hot, I leapt over her and shifted in mid-air to dodge one of the airborne doors, landing on my feet once more.

Her wings stretched out wide enough to gather the hypnotised Doloreans and propel them against the far wall, the stage, and even the bannister of the stairs. Ever heard of the term 'Wingspan'? Well, that move was called a 'Wingslam'! And yes, from my books. Best purchase ever, right? A bit of an extreme manoeuvre, but at least it didn't kill anyone. At the most, it might've fractured a few of their bones, but nothing that wouldn't heal with a quick visit to Guy's place.

On Rudy's back was the one who approved of the mad battle tactic. Rick dismounted from Rudy and made a beeline to check up on me.

"I'm good, thanks," I assured Rick. "Cheers, Rudy!" I shouted to my Questing Beast.

Rudy would've cawed victoriously and rushed to my side, but she wasn't really herself currently. Upon her turning around, I realised that Valentin had started up his song again. Rudy's eyes were cold, dead, and they were locked on me.

"Rudy, it's me," I said delicately. "It's Corbé. You know, your best friend? I know you. You don't want to- Holy shit!"

I snatched Rick out of the air as I ran away from the hulking teal mass of dragon barreling for me.

Sukawww! Rudy screamed, expanding her wings as she lumbered behind me with her jaws snapping.

The second that I stepped out of the Secret Cathedral to avoid getting eaten up by Rudy, I was sucked into the ground.

Rudy pecked at the ground that I was swallowed into until she was convinced that I wasn't coming back. She faced her conductor and approached him emptyhandedly. Emptywingedly? Hmm.

"Everyone get up!" Valentin ordered the Doloreans, them rising shakily. "Get back to it and pick up the pace before Corbé shows up again."

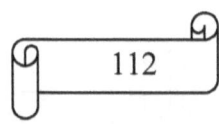

As the Doloreans got back in line to speedily give up their belongings, Valentin stared out the door, wondering where I had disappeared off to.

Within a pocket of air just beneath the dungeon level of the castle, I found myself sitting next to Snapback and Black Silver.

"Corbé!" Snapback, dressed in a tuxedo, cheered as he rushed me with a hug.

"Well, you look dashing," I told Snapback.

"Thanks," He smiled. "I was going to go to the ball, but I showed up late."

"No, you arrived just on time," I assured him.

"By the looks of things, yeah," He said.

"The situation 'tis hardly ideal, nay," Black Silver added.

"Why are you here Master Silver?" I asked.

"The Fiend above may control anyone he desires, dost thou wish to do battle with me, Apprentice Corbé?" Black Silver poised a brow, placing a hand on his sheathed sword's hilt.

"Fair point. He already has control over Rudy," I informed.

"I believe 'tis time to give thee thine final lesson in the dark Witch-Crafts to aid in this battle," Black Silver stood up properly.

"Well, I…"

Wait, if I already know Life, Creation, Naturalisation, Manipulation, and Destruction, then that only leaves…

"Whoahoho, no," I asserted. "I am *not* killing Valentin. He might be causing problems, but he's a good person."

"Apprentice Corbé, dost thou trust me?"

"Of course," I said unflinchingly. "But I don't see how-"

"Then thou must do as I do."

With those words, Black Silver drew out the Death Spell. It was a large circle with a line down it, three lines below that symbolised the skull's teeth, and swirled eyes.

"Death magic 'tis fickle and powerful, thou must desire and be willing to end one's existence. Whereas thou hast created Lady Rick with love in thine heart, thee must focus only on ending one's life with thine pure hatred. Raw. Unadulterated. A hatred that…" Black Silver stared at me, his Spell dissolving the eye contact barrier between us. "… I do not believe to reside within thee."

"I don't hate him, Master Silver," I said. "I might not've known him for long, but neither have I for Rick," I looked to my Sprite who

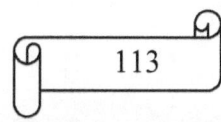

shared my discomfort of the utilisation of the Death Spell. "Rick's my friend... Valentin's my friend... I'm not going to kill him."

"Thou must try," Black Silver urged. "Goodman Valentin be up yonder thieving and with the type of hatred that *can* end thine life if thou pushes him too far. Thine kingdom's future depends on how thou chooses to dispatch this threat."

"Sorry if that's not really striking the right chord for me," I informed.

As I tried to focus on finding another way out, Rick seemed to have gotten an idea from my words since she proceeded to urgently tug on my shoulder strap.

"What? What is it?" I asked.

Rick mimed playing Valentin's golden flute. It took no time for me to realise what she was getting at.

"... Striking the right chord... That's it!" I gleefully held Rick's tiny hands, turning to Black Silver. "I don't have to put an end to Valetnin, I just need to put an end to his song."

"Whate'er thou wishes to do, 'tis advised to conduct it swiftly," Black Silver said.

"Will do, but I do need some help," I said.

"How?" Snapback asked.

"I need you to get me into position, and from you," I turned to my master. "I need your sword."

Valentin monitored the open doorway, vigilantly looking for me to make my entrance. As he impatiently stood there, Colby climbed up onto Valentin's shoulder and nestled against his neck. He delicately stroked the rat with a sigh.

"I guess you're coming with me to Shroudolous?" Valentin asked to the rodent with him squeaking positively.

"When you get there, tell Valaeria I said, 'ellooo!" I shouted from the opposite balcony.

Valentin, Colby, Rudy, and all of the zombie Doloreans faced me, swinging my master's sword and biting my thumb alongside Rick who was doing likewise.

"Corbé!" The Fiend barked.

"Val!" I kiddingly returned.

With Black Silver's sword, I cut the netting that contained all of the balloons. Gripping the rope, I leapt off of the balcony to swing down towards Valentin's position. A wall of balloons was heading the

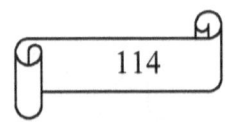

Fiend's way with Rick and I riding it along which compelled him to play his flute, taking direct control over Rudy.

The Questing Beast beat her wings hard at the huge netting of balloons, popping near all of the balls of helium at once due to the instant pressure.

I swiftly produced a shield to soften my collision with the stage once my swinging manoeuvre was over. Quickly, I scrambled to get up and headed up the stairs to get to Valentin. Rick and I zipped past the Doloreans who were holding their heads as if nursing headaches, gripping their sides in pain, or falling over due to broken knees. As for the rats, their mind control vanished and so did they, skedaddling away but leaving their thieving bags. The only rodent that remained was Colby.

Valentin played his pipe to recall the vermin, but this time it was different. The sound that came out was higher and distorted. The Fiend buffed the lip plate and tried again with the same result.

"What did you do?" Valentin squeaked at me with a voice four octaves higher than his normal tone.

I had to stifle my laughter as I got onto Valentin's level.

Helium, I smirked. *You got to love it. I've got about a minute before this wears off.*

With Black Silver's sword in hand, I charged at Valentin. I wasn't angling to try to lob his head off, rather I was trying to break his flute. As for Rick, her job was to zip around him and try to get it if I couldn't manage to smash it. Valentin was light on his feet, able to dodge out of the way of my Orbit of Mars manoeuvre. Every time I gave a heavy swing, he'd either duck under or leap back.

Since it wasn't proving beneficial, I decided to go with the Dance of Pele. Encircling the Fiend, I took my jabs at the flute, but my moves were hindered by my reluctance to hurt him. Valentin was aware of this so he kept the fife behind his back at all times.

Rick hovered around him and now had a firm grip on it, but the Fiend's was tighter.

As for Colby, he crawled down Valentin's arm and was now hissing and biting at Rick.

This isn't working, I mentally moaned. *Time for Odin's Judgement… Hopefully he's fast enough to block it.*

I did a backflip away from Valentin to give myself some distance and did my charge jump at him, hoisting my blade over my head. On my way to Valentin, the world slowed down. The Fiend didn't make

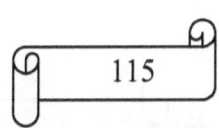

the obvious move of blocking with his flute. Rather, with a look of surrender, he accepted and shut his eyes.

Val...

My arms' strength stifled, but my swing was already on its way towards Valentin. I couldn't stop the manoeuvre no matter how much I wanted to. However, before it made contact with Valentin, Colby tackled the blade's side to knock it out of my hand. It was a heroic move, but one that left the rat on the floor in a growing puddle of his own blood.

"O god," I recoiled in shock.

"Colby!" Valentin rushed to the rat.

I dropped Black Silver's sword and pulled at my hair.

"I'm so sorry!" I woefully apologised. "I... I think I can help..." I joined Valentin's side. "Black Silver taught me how to-"

"VALENTIN!" The booming authoritative voice came from the entrance to the Secret Cathedral.

Standing across the way from us was the Shroudolous priestess herself, Valaeria. With her arrival and exclamation, an uneasiness settled in my stomach upon my sudden revelation. A revelation that Valentin shared. Our voices were back to normal.

Faster than I could act, Valentin scooped up Colby, leapt off of the balcony, and played his fife as he landed on the stage. Instantly, Valaeria took to his song.

O flock no...

I tried to make a break for it, but a long shadow claw that originated from Valaeria snagged me by my waist. As it retracted, I gripped onto the bannister to anchor myself down.

Rick hovered over the extended arm, drawing out a Destruction Spell of fire. With a swift punch, the claw's wrist burst into black smog and broke me free.

"Cheers, Rick," I said, holding my side.

Now that I knew it was coming, I was able to dodge out of the way of Valaeria's subsequent arm lunge attacks.

Whereas Rick used destruction, I chose to use Creation. It more or less did the same job.

Although Valentin was controlling her, judging from the look on the Priestess' face, she was resisting but not enough to ceasefire. From the corner of my eye, I could see a cluster of rainbow colour heading for the exit.

"Take care of her!" I ordered Rick.

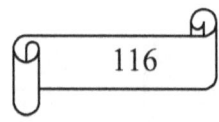

The Sprite nodded, manifesting a solar flare of strung together Spells that she used to whip away Valaeria's shadow limbs.

I cartwheeled off to the side, carving a Creation Spell in my hand. Upon landing, I shot the Spell quickly followed by a Naturalisation leaf, instructing it to form a wall of fire in front of the merchant.

"Val!" I shouted at him as Rick and I dodged Valaeria's attacks. "You need to stop! You don't need to steal anything from anyone!"

"I don't care about that anymore!" Valentin barked at me, staring down at the weak rodent caressed in his arms. "I just want to leave! Please, just let me leave, Corbé!"

"I don't give up on friends that easily," I stood firmly.

"Fine… Then you have to deal with *these* friends of yours," Valentin placed his flute at his mouth, playing his song.

From the crowd of Doloreans, only a few of them advanced, but it was the few that counted the most to me. Guy, Rudy, Gladys, and Tes all emerged in battle ready stances.

"Please, Val, don't do this," I pleaded, getting myself prepped to fight regardless with my aura armaments in hand.

"You're the one who's always talking about friends. Maybe you shouldn't have so many," Valentin said.

Just before anyone could make an advance, the ground trembled. Two loud battle cries came from the entrance. Both bassy, one of a man and one avian. Through the wall of fire leapt out Black Silver and Snapback with molten skin. Black Silver placed his hand on the floor which recalled his ivory blade from the shadows so he was armed to fight.

"Holy Grail," I choked in my throat.

Everyone charged me at once.

Focus, Corbé. Deal with the big threats first.

After forming an aura barrier, I sent it Black Silver's way and leapt at Rudy. By sliding down her back Flintstones style, I reached her tail.

Sorry, Rudy, but instincts conquer mind control!

I vigorously scratched Rudy's tail and quickly leapt off of her.

With an irritated squawk, my Questing Beast swirled around in a circle, whipping her tail against Guy, Tes, and Gladys and slamming them into the buffet table.

Four down, two to go.

Black Silver managed to break through my barrier and was now heading my way.

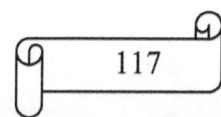

As quickly as I could possibly draw, I crafted dozens upon dozens of Shield-Spells to launch at my master. They would launch and latch onto his armour, sending him back a few feet. However, the more I made the more they piled up until Black Silver was completely covered in a dome of shields and unable to move.

Something tells me that that's not going to hold him for long, I warned myself.

As for Snapback, he was currently in his Burning Phoenix mode so getting close to him wasn't a real option. However, there was a simple fix for the little Burrowing Eagle. The Grinoff swung his flaming fists at me as I backed away and dodged with every attack.

With reluctance, I drew out a Manipulation Spell and let my aura take over Snapback. With a gentle tugging motion away from him, I syphoned off Snapback's fiery exterior to revert him back to normal. Although that got rid of *that* problem, I still had a jacked eagle trying to kill me.

Off to the side, Rudy had gotten over her tail's itching, Guy, Gladys, and Tes, were back on their feet, and Valaeria was getting more furious in her assault against Rick who was frantically trying to hold her own.

This is getting out of hand, I thought to myself. *If I don't do anything fast someone's going to get hurt... or worse...*

I looked to my master, cracking the surface of his forcefield entrapment.

Sooner or later you're going to have to fight him head on or... The thought of taking Black Silver's advice sent an uneasy tremor throughout my mind and body. *I've never killed anyone before... but I don't want anyone else dying on my watch...*

With a lamenting and regretful glance at my new Fiendish friend, I'd made up my mind just as Black Silver broke free.

Valentin... I am so sorry...

As if my body was born to cast such a charm, the skull shape for the Death Spell was formed in my palm. All that was left to do was send it Valentin's way.

Danke, Val, for being my friend.

With a cry filled shriek, I hurled the Spell across the Secret Cathedral, the scarlet skull imbedding itself into the Fiend's ribcage. All at once, every single standing body in the building hit the floor.

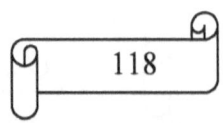

I dropped to my knees, exhausted, tired, and emotionally drained. A titanic sinking feeling took over my heart, growing into a sharp, cold pain all through my limbs and brain.

My hands reached up to my head to remove my beret. No thoughts, no words, nothing passed through my mind except the image of my guilt-ridden face reflected in the beret's obsidian badge.

An aura of warmth presented itself to me in the form of Rick, placing her hand on my shoulder. The sourest bittersweet smile was presented to the world upon my face. Wordlessly, Rick took her eyes off of me to look at the landscape of freed Doloreans as if to say, 'It was at a cost, but you saved the day.'

"Thanks, Rick," I rubbed my lower eyelids to prevent them from spilling with tears.

In an awkward attempt to be supportive, Rick tried to locate the most appropriate spot to give me a hug. She eventually decided my forearm was the best place.

My return hug was interrupted by a moan in the room. It didn't come from Black Silver, or Tes, or Guy, or Gladys... but from...

"V-V..." I rose from the golden floor, placing my beret back on and wiping my eyes. "V-Valentin?"

Rick and I rushed across the cathedral, joining the Fiend's side on the floor.

"Valentin? Val?!" I shook the merchant frantically. "You're alive?! How can you be alive?! I mean, I'm ecstatic that you are, but... HOW?"

"Hast thou forgotten?" Black Silver coughed, using his sword to rise from the scorched and slippery ground. "Thine Death Spell requires a breed of hate and darkness to reside within thine heart... Thou hast none to give."

I processed my master's words for a moment, realising what this meant.

"You... You knew that my Death Spell wouldn't kill Val."

"Aye," Black Silver weakly nodded.

Valentin groggily sat up, automatically gaining my attention.

"What happened?" He seemed out of it only momentarily before his face contorted into one of urgency. "Colby!" Valentin exclaimed.

He faced his rat that was lying next to him and barely breathing.

"You said there was a way to help him," Valentin turned to me. "How?"

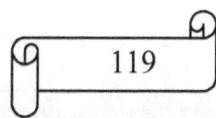

"Master Silver," I faced Black Silver who only gave me a single nod as if saying, 'You know what to do'. "Well," I looked between Valentin and Colby, facing the former finally with a weak and hopeful grin. "Just… give your friend a hug."

Without question and yet carefully, Valentin scooped up Colby and looked into his weak eyes before holding the blood-soaked rat to his chest. An aurora of light flashed around Valentin which confirmed what I suspected would happen. However, by the time Valentin opened his arms, Colby vanished.

"Colby?" Valentin asked in a fluster.

He searched the area for his rat until he felt a twitch at his side, and then one on his back, and then his neck until it reached his shoulder and the brave little rat was found on the Fiend's shoulder.

"You little scheisse!" Valentin ruffled Colby's fur on the top of his head. "What did you do? What did *I* do?" He asked me.

"That, my dear apprentice, is what's called Spirit Healing," I said sophisticatedly.

"Spirit Healing," Valentin repeated in awe. "I love it!"

"I figured you would," I giggled. "Sorry for almost killing you by the way."

"Likewise," Valentin offered a hand to shake.

I gripped his palm tightly and threw it towards me to fling him into a laugh filled embrace.

"I suppose attempted murder isn't the worst thing that someone can do in this kingdom," I justified, glancing over at Tes who was only just now getting up.

Footsteps down the way peeled my eyes off of my court jester, giving me a broad smile.

"Speaking of which, Tes," I called from my spot.

"Hmm?" The jester massaged her head.

"Your date's here," I gestured to the entrance.

"My date?" Tes looked over at the latecomer.

"What the flaming Hell did I miss?" Lancelot asked.

The ex-king was clean shaven, bathed, dressed in a three-piece suit of red and black, and was looking at all the unconscious Doloreans and still burning fires.

"Lancelot!" Tes beamed.

The jester got up and speedily tiptoed between resting mind control victims to reach her love.

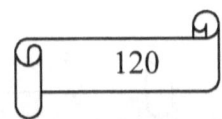

"What are you doing out?" Tes asked as she hugged and kissed Lancelot repeatedly. "Did Corbé release you already?"

"No, but she is a woman of her word," Lancelot looked to me. "Everyone in Dolorous was invited to this ball."

I got up and crouched down next to Guy, lightly slapping him awake.

"Psst, rise and shine. We need you to play a song for the happy couple," I told him, helping him get up.

Guy glanced over at Lancelot and Tes, sighed, and reluctantly went to go retrieve his guitar and microphone.

As the two of them took to the centre of the dance floor and swayed together, Colby tapped Rick's shoulder and offered a paw to her. She glanced around in confusion as if the rodent was trying to communicate with someone else. After an era of sheepishness, Rick took Colby's paw so the two of them could dance alongside Tes and Lancelot.

I stood back and watched with a grin. It wasn't the party I was expecting, but then again this wasn't the life I was expecting to lead a month ago either. All things considered, the night turned up Le Fay after all. As my gaze passed over the Cathedral, I spotted the remnants of my anti-ageing potion on the floor. Valentin noticed my disheartened expression and joined my side.

"What was that?" He asked, looking at the pool of potion.

"That was supposed to be the thing to stop me from ageing," I said. "I apparently age one year a day, so I'm probably going to die in two months, so cheers," I gave a shrug.

Valentin contemplated on what to do until he spotted his flute on the floor.

"You know," He picked it up and twirled it amongst his fingers. "This thing's caused a lot of trouble, but maybe…" He poised it to his lips as he faced me. "I can do some good with it."

Valentin's song played like before, but instead of being mind controlled, a sort of Ever Chill level of cold coated my body before easing off of me.

"Umm, Val? What did you do?" I inspected myself, finding that nothing had changed.

"Hopefully it's not what I did, it's what I made you *not* do," Valentin approached me. "If my powers work the way I think they do, you won't age any faster than anyone else, more or less."

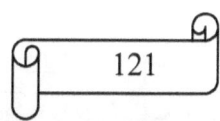

"Really? O thank you!" I rushed Valentin with another hug. "Did you want to dance?"

"Nein, I need to be heading home. We, I mean," Valentin glanced at his dancing rodent friend. "Plus, I need to wipe everyone's minds of me and what's happened."

"You don't have to, you know. I was talking to a few of these people during the ball and they really liked my outfit. You're a talented tailor, you just need to show your confidence. You don't have to wipe their memories of you…" I looked to Lancelot and Tes as they stared lovingly into each other's eyes during their waltz. "Sometimes even the craziest of second chances can happen."

"YOU!"

All conscious eyes turned to the enraged and awakened Priestess of Fiends. Valentin and I bumped into each other, trying to get in front to guard the other.

"Uhhh, maybe just one person needs to forget what's happened," I nervously laughed, propping Valentin's flute up to his mouth.

Before Valaeria could snag at Valentin with her demon claws, her face fell into a dreary state.

"Ja, maybe we can try again next year," Valentin shrugged, pocketing his flute. "Thank you, though. Maybe one day I can play for you as a true piper and you as a true queen," He bowed.

"One day," I smiled. "That'd be great, but until then…"

I unhooked my friendship bracelet from my wrist to clip onto Valentin's.

"A little something to remember me by," I gave the Fiend a wink.

"I could never forget *you*," Valentin grinned, giving me one last hug. "My friend, Corbé Le Fay."

With a little help from my friends, I was able to cart and sort everyone away into their homes. Black Silver repaired the doors to the Secret Cathedral so I could reseal it after which he told me to meet him just outside of the kingdom.

"Come on, Rick," I patted the Sprite who rested on my shoulder.

Just as I locked up the Cathedral, I faced towards the staircase to find a tremendously flummoxed Aderyn.

"I'm assuming I'm really late," Raiden asked, rubbing the back of his neck.

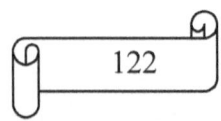

"It's a long storey," I said, slowly approaching my adviser nonchalantly. "I'm actually glad that you didn't make it. I wouldn't have wanted you to get hurt."

"Get hurt? What happ-?"

"Rai," I placed a finger on his lips with an eyeroll, using my freehand to place his hand on my waist.

I positioned my hands on his shoulders as we proceeded to dance with each other in the centre of the true love statue hedges.

"Better late than never," I said.

"I suppose so," Raiden chuckled.

In my mind, there was music playing, swelling, and resonating, but within Raiden's mind something else was going on, I could tell.

"Corbé, I need to tell you something…" Raiden let out a reluctant breath.

"What's that?" I asked cautiously.

"That talk we had in the Cathedral… Where I asked you to the ball…" Raiden let go of me and stepped back, reaching into his pocket. "It wasn't me, it was this thing," He flaunted a glowing lariat in his palm. "It's an artefact I bought in town… This is my 'confidence'."

… Raiden…

At first, I wanted to get angry at him, but after a night of mind control, fighting, and emotional ups and downs this seemed like a little blip on my mental radar.

"Raiden… You're a lot like Valentin," I said. "You two might think that you need a miracle to give yourselves what you want, but you just need to be confident in what you know. You know plenty of things that make me happy and smile and love being your friend, you don't *have* to always be my adviser. You can just be Raiden Aderyn."

"You say be confident, but how am I supposed to do that? I just don't know," Raiden gripped his lariat tightly.

"All you need to do is believe in yourself…" I stepped up to Raiden, placing a hand on his cheek. "… as much as I believe in you."

I gave Raiden a peck on his forehead before heading towards the exit.

"I gotta go meet with Black Silver. Good night, Raiden," I said.

Before my foot could be placed on the first step of the staircase, Raiden called out, "Corbé."

I looked over my shoulder to the Aderyn son, his confidence artefact placed at the base of the King Arthur statue.

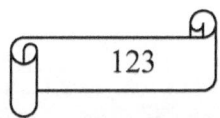

"Did you want to come over tomorrow night?" Raiden asked, keeping a steady pace so to not have his voice crack.

I faced forward, squinting at him quizzically.

"We could cook some pastries, read some books," Raiden offered. "Ooh, you can finally see how my telescope works!" He said with eagerness.

That's my boy.

"So?" Raiden fiddled with his ring. "What do you say?" He asked.

"I say…" I folded my arms and turned around to walk upstairs. "See you then. Happy Valentine's Day!"

"Yeah," Raiden giddily grinned as he watched me go. "Happy Valentine's Day."

"Master Silver, where are we going?" I asked my mentor as we headed to the edge of the cavern wall of Dolorous on the backs of our rides and with Rick on my shoulder.

"A place that thee must behold," Black Silver said.

Seeing as Black Silver was being vague, I sort of assumed that he wouldn't give me any more details.

Upon meeting the base of the wall, Black Silver dismounted from Cath to draw his blade from its scabbard. He lightly ran its tip along the rock surface. From the arch that he drew was a doorway that Black Silver welcomed me through.

"After thee," Black Silver said.

"Stay here," I told Rudy as I dismounted her.

With Black Silver and Cath, I entered the unknown hidden cave. A rainbow colour basked the three of us as we headed further and deeper into the tunnel. At its distant end, it opened up to a large cavern. There was a patch of dirt pushed into the corner, a king-sized bed set in mahogany, the floor was littered with half opened crates, and its walls were like a hive's with dozens upon dozens of circular holes in them. However, the hive texture was attributed to the mason jars that made up the room. The rainbow light came from the hundreds of different coloured Sprites that were flying all over the room but staying up high. Some of them were sitting on the wooden crates, retrieving sugar plums and nectar to nosh down on.

Rick and I beheld the room with the same level of amazement.

"This is where they go," I said in awe of all the Sprites. "Are these Sprites from all of your previous Apprentices?"

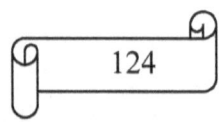

"Nay, only a fair portion. The other Masters allow them to live here with me. Gawain's Sprite be here as well."

"Go ahead," I motioned for Rick to go have fun with her fellow Sprites for a while to which she did.

Black Silver stepped over to his bed and took a seat, facing the far wall away from me. He ran his sword against the wall like before to reveal a mannequin meant for armour. After popping his back and clearing his throat, Black Silver removed his helmet and placed it upon the mannequin.

I sort of grimaced at the thought of seeing Black Silver's face since I'd never seen it before, but when he faced me I couldn't stop staring. His silver eyes were like his bright white teeth and his skin was darker than his pitch black armour. His sterling hair fell to his shoulders and caught the light off of his Sprites like a rainbow vignette.

Whoa...

For some reason, I never thought I'd ever actually see Black Silver's face. He seemed like that sort of mysterious celestial being that sort of didn't exist while existing at the same time. A quantum being of some kind. However, even though Black Silver was right there in front of me, his entire presence was like a living shadow. Solid enough to be something, but obscure enough to assume that my hand could pass through him like smoke.

"Hast thou assumed that I may not be mortal?" Black Silver asked, removing his gauntlets and chest plate to reveal a silver tunic underneath.

"Honestly, yeah," I said blatantly.

"Apprentice Corbé, I wish for thee to do something."

After him removing his armour and placing it onto his mannequin, he rose from his bed and approached me.

"What's that?" I asked him.

My master stood in front of me and puffed his chest out.

"Place thine ear upon mine breast," Black Silver said.

"A-all right..." I spoke softly.

I inched closer to Black Silver, got on my tiptoes, and nestled my head between his muscly toned pecs. It was like pressing myself against a cold stone only slightly submerged in water. Beyond the strange feeling of my master's body, I could hear the churning of his blood, the exhalations of his lungs, and the slow thudding of his heart.

"I may perish like any mortal of this world. I am imperfect. I feel like any other," I felt Black Silver's words as they vibrated throughout his chest.

I separated from him and looked him in his sterling eyes.

"I am thine master, aye, howbeit I am also merely a man. I shall ne'er allow thee to do something thou art nigh at peace in doing," Black Silver assured me. "If thou trust me."

I took a step away from my master and held out my forearm for a Roman style handshake. Black Silver accepted the gesture with a smile on his face, the one I always imagined he wore when content but now was visible.

"I trust you," I said without a shred of doubt in my voice.

"Most excellent," Black Silver nodded. "In which, thine trust shall be rewarded... with this..."

Black Silver stepped over to the portion of the wall next to his standing armour. He ran his sword along the surface to reveal a second mannequin but this one was for a woman. It was a majority black suit of armour with black mail joints, ruby blades on the forearms, shins, and similar spikes on the knees, shoulders, and elbows. A red waist cape was fastened onto the armour which had several flechettes and arrows holstered into it. On its chest there was similar cryptic text to Black Silver's which I had yet to learn how to read.

"This..." I spoke in near inaudible whispers. "This is for me?"

"Aye," Black Silver placed a hand on my shoulder and directed me towards the mannequin. "Once thee becomes an official knight."

We approached the armour with me in a gobsmacked state, staring into the eyeholes of the Tudor helmet as I imagined one day wearing it.

"The armour be to thine liking?" My master asked me.

"It's perfect," I swooned.

Although I had an animosity towards the colour red, I wouldn't want the suit to change one bit.

"Howe'er, for now..." Black Silver clapped his hands.

All at once, a flock of Sprites flew down to me to plate pieces of silver armour onto my shoulders and legs. The pauldrons around my shoulders were accented with two slits on each that produced red light. As for the greaves, they ended in scarlet sabatons that came to dangerous points.

"Thou may don these for thine future adventures," Black Silver said.

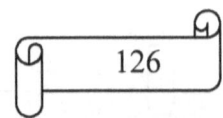

"This is so unbelievably awesome!" I rushed Black Silver with an extremely unprofessional hug. "Thank you, Master Silver."

Black Silver laughed as he wrapped his arms around me.

"Thou art so very welcome, Apprentice Corbé."

Once he released me, I stared at my future suit of armour.

"Dost thou feel prepared for the future?" Black Silver asked.

Rick hovered by my shoulder with a plum in her hands, grinning as if to be asking the same question to me.

With a long-drawn breath and closed eyes, a broad, confident, and cocky smile grew on my face. I opened my eyes with my irises glowing crimson as I spoke, "Verily."

Epilogue: Dealing With Death

"Night, mum," Raiden kissed his mother goodnight once the two of them entered the Aderyn household.

"Goodnight, sweetheart," Gladys said, veering towards the kitchen to cook herself up a tasty late-night snack.

The young Aderyn boy almost tripped on his way up the stairs. He slung his jacket over his shoulder, undid the first few buttons on his dress shirt, and unbuckled his neck ornament so it'd dangle freely.

Raiden opened his bedroom door with a big breathy yawn. He lied himself in his bed and repositioned to be on his side. His thoughts on his current relationship status with Corbé and anticipation for tomorrow night almost eclipsed something off about his room. Almost.

He sat straight up when he realised that his entire room had been cleaned up, gaping hole in the roof and all. The chemicals on his desk had been rearranged, his papers had been reorganised into labelled files, and his books had all been alphabetised.

"Mum," Raiden rose from his mattress. "Did you-?"

The door being slammed shut in front of Raiden halted him verbally and physically. Standing before the young Aderyn was a slender pale man with wavy grey hair, hazel eyes, and was dressed in a black and grey pinstriped suit. The stranger was holding a gold pocket watch whose face had been shattered, inspecting the fictional time that the broken clock kept.

"Raiden Ouroboros Aderyn," The man near death said, pocketing his watch and looking the boy over quizzically. "Late as usual."

"Wh-who are you?" Raiden backed away from the man who loomed over him.

The boy glanced over at his satchel hung up on his coatrack which contained his weapon of choice.

"They call me Death, the Reaper, the Slayer of All, but my name's Grim. Charmed, I'm sure," Grim grinned.

"You're a Reaper? D-does that mean-?"

"You're not dying, not yet. You should know that you're not *that* lucky, Raiden."

"Then why are you here?" Raiden asked, inching closer to his bag.

"Because I need something from you."

Grim backed the young Aderyn against his coatrack which sprung the boy into action. He swiftly reached into his bag to retrieve his crossbow, but ended up pulling out a tree branch shaped like said

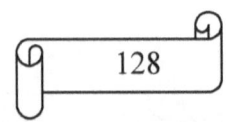

crossbow. Once more, the target for the crossbow wasn't there anymore.

"What the…?"

Raiden scanned the room. Upon the second sweep of the bedroom he found Grim sitting at the desk, leafing through Raiden's personal notes on custom potions. In Grim's lap was the crossbow that Raiden intended to pull out.

"Fascinating brews you've come up with. I'm rather into potions myself," Grim said, reading the ingredients for Cinder Thorn Poison. "You really do have a head on your shoulders, don't you?"

"I-I guess…" Raiden clutched the branch to use it as a weapon in the event he'd need one. "I'd like to keep it on my shoulders if you don't mind."

"No promises," Grim said.

"Did you just come here to talk to me about potions?"

"No, not potions," Grim placed the book away to give Raiden his undivided attention. "Cartography."

"Cartog…? You want a map?" Raiden squinted at the Reaper.

"Yes, a very specific map. One of the Medis kingdom of Idem and one that doubles as a portal *to* it," Grim said.

"Y-you… I-I…" Raiden lowered the branch so he could scratch his head in his confusion. "Why?"

"I promise, the details are a different storey within itself. Let's keep it at: Someone I know needs it and soon. How quickly do you think you could make one?"

"I don't know," Raiden folded his arms, keeping his distance from the stranger. "It'd take a while. I'd need to know the layout of the place and I've never been outside of Dolorous before."

"Would the process go faster if you were there?"

"In theory…" Raiden cautiously answered.

"Give me an estimate on the finishing date," Grim delicately ordered.

"I guess," Raiden rubbed his neck. "Six months at a minimum."

"Six months?"

"The map drawing won't take any time at all, it's just infusing it with enough trans-dimensional energy to form a portal would take a while," He explained. "Not to mention collecting the necessary ingredients to do so."

"Using what method?"

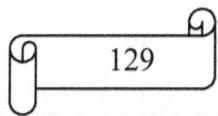

"Submerging the scroll in a dimensional resin so it can soak it in on a molecular level," Raiden said.

"Have you heard of Origoma."

"Uh…" Raiden bit the corner of his lip, trying to recall if the term was familiar.

"Origoma is a type of magical origami used by the people of Atlantis. By following the folds and imbuing certain energies into it, it might be a viable way to form the required portal."

"If you know all this, why don't you just do it?" Raiden asked.

"Because, I don't have any magical powers currently. My abilities are derived off of a mixture of potions I've learned to make over the years."

"I don't have any magical powers either," Raiden shrugged.

"I beg to differ. You have more power than you could ever brew up into a potion, power that could rival gods, power that I hope you use to help me out. One day, who knows, Death might just owe you a favour."

The words of the Reaper resonated with the Aderyn boy on a deeper level than Grim intended. Raiden loosened his grip on the tree branch and sat himself back onto his bed.

"How long am I going to be gone for? My mum is going to wonder if I'm missing for too long."

"Only a couple of hours for the trip and I'll pop back in to pick up the map once you're done," Grim said. "Besides, I don't think that it's your mother that you're so concerned about missing you."

Raiden thought over the Reaper's offer until coming up with a thought.

"An artefact merchant in town was telling me about a super powerful and incredibly rare item that he didn't have on hand," Raiden started.

"Go on," Grim said with a sort of knowing tone to his voice.

"It's called a Gall-O-Wisp," The Aderyn said. "If you want me to do this, you have to find me one."

"A Gall-O-Wisp, huh? What exactly are you going to do with one of those?" Grim asked.

"I feel like you already know the answer to that… Deal?"

It was Grim's turn to think matters over. As he thought, he took out his pocket watch to adjust the time to three o'clock before putting it back into his pocket.

Grim rose from his seat and went to the door.

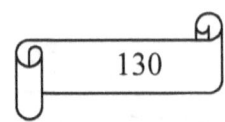

"I suppose I'll be right back," Grim said, giving the Aderyn a smirk upon his exit.

The second that the door shut behind the Reaper, Raiden woke up in his bed. His entire room was in shambles, his papers were strewn all over the floor, his beakers and test tubes were a Kaleidoscope of mismatched colours, and his books were all out of order. Just the way Raiden had left it. The Aderyn shivered from the cold entering his room from the hole in the roof. On Raiden's bed next to him was his oversized crossbow that he had intended to pull on Grim.

Before Raiden could question whether or not he *was* visited by Death, he spotted the one thing that seemed out of place. On his desk was a note written on a glowing white piece of paper. It wasn't a letter to Raiden, it was more of a transcript starting from 'Raiden Ouroboros Aderyn' and ending in 'I suppose I'll be right back'. At the bottom of the transcript was the symbol of the black sun as if it was a signature.

"Jeesh," Raiden rolled his eyes as he undressed for bed and laid down. "Mediterraneans."

"Tonight was delightful," Lancelot complimented Corbé's Valentine's day festivity as the two of them sauntered down the stairs to the dungeon, the former in his usual handcuffs.

"You should've been there earlier," Corbé told Lancelot. "Not like I didn't have everything under control."

"Naturally," The ex-king chortled in his throat. "Things went off the rails again, didn't they?"

"That's usually how Dolorean life goes, aye," Corbé nodded, reaching into her cape pocket to retrieve the dungeon keys, revealing the barren cells within the depths of the castle.

"What was it this time?" Lancelot asked.

"Just a flute player who could mind control people," Corbé informed.

"Hmm, and he wasn't able to control you?"

"He was, but I managed to break free. So, if in future you think you can brainwash me, you've got another thing coming," Corbé lightly warned.

"It wasn't on my agenda," Lancelot said. "However, that is quite interesting. If I were to wager a guess, I'd assume that it's due to your-"

"Tenacity? Stick-to-itiveness? Bodacity?" Corbé offered.

"I was going to say Birthright," Lancelot laughed.

"Birthright? Like the fact that I'm a Le Fay?" Corbé asked.

"Not in the way you're assuming, no," Lancelot said. "Being a Le Fay *does* make you a royal, but being a Le Fay within itself is special because of that," The ex-king faced Corbé, gesturing to the natural symbol branded into the little Le Fay's cheek. "That is a Birthright. There are a few Birthrights that exist, all being symbolised upon the flesh of the Birthright bearers. Beings like the Seer have the Birthright on their wrist, the one who bears the Condor's Wings has it on their chest, but the Wicked's Claw is upon the face. All of them can be passed on to whoever the bearer chooses and whoever can handle it."

"Handle it in what way?"

"When one has a Birthright, it welcomes the light as well as the darkness into their life. Only the strong-willed can survive having a Birthright. If you weren't worthy of being queen, you would've been killed by that brand alone by now. I noticed it the first day I met you, but I feel like I was in denial back then."

Lancelot and Corbé arrived at the proper cell and the ex-king took the liberty of opening and placing himself into his room.

"One of these days you're going to make a wonderful queen, whenever you feel ready," Lancelot said, shutting the door between Corbé and himself.

"You're not just kissing up to me because I've got these are you?" Corbé jangled the keys in front of her face after locking Lancelot into his cell.

"No, I know no matter what I say or do you'll always resent me for what I've done. Since my body won't be free anytime soon, I figured the truth would set at least my soul free. It really has. You are a formidable foe and an impending benevolent sovereign. If you become queen…" Lancelot held a vacant stare which seemed to make him chortle. "*When* you become queen, I hope it's a day that I'm free to see."

Lancelot gave the Le Fay a warm smile before turning away and heading towards his bed.

"Thank you again for tonight, Corbé."

Although the ex-sovereign was making himself comfortable in his rinky-dink accommodations, Corbé didn't share in the comfort. Something itched at her as she fondled the keys that she still had in her hand. Lancelot stilled his breathing in an attempt to achieve his slumber sooner.

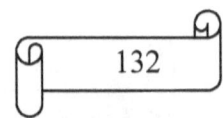

Against all forms of better judgement, Corbé unlocked the cell which didn't cause Lancelot to react immediately. However, the sound of footsteps approaching and shuffling cards enticed him into opening an eye to Corbé.

"You like card games?" Corbé asked as she sat herself down, riffling the cards.

"King Balin and I often partook in Tarot Fate with each other," Lancelot rose from his lying position to sit on the edge of his bed. "We would play until we got bored and just started to tell each other storeys about the pictures on the cards."

"That sounds cute," Corbé giggled.

"For lack of a better term, I suppose," Lancelot half-shrugged with a grin.

Lancelot squinted at the backs of the cards Corbé was shuffling, their backs seemed to be brick walls in design.

"You probably haven't played this game before," Corbé said. "Actually, I *know* you haven't played this game before. I tried to teach the Aderyns, but they fell asleep on me in the middle of me explaining the rules."

"So, there *is* something that that Aderyn boy isn't good at," Lancelot jabbed at Raiden.

"Do you think you can fair better?"

"Almost certainly," Lancelot said confidently.

"Fine then," Corbé said, placing the cards down to take up the keys one more time. "Prove it."

Corbé unlocked the anti-magic handcuffs to allow Lancelot's hands freedom once again. The most freedom that they'd ever seen in the past month. Lancelot massaged his wrists once he placed the handcuffs off to the side. His hands were unbound, Corbé was distracted by organising the cards into multiple piles, and the cell door was wide open. However, Lancelot never once glanced at the gateway to his liberation. He instead took a seat in front of Corbé on the floor. Lancelot poised his hand on his chin to observe Corbé's process of dealing out all of the cards.

"What's this game called?" Lancelot asked.

"I like to call it Clockwork Towers," Corbé beamed.

"Clockwork Towers," Lancelot repeated in his fascination.

"Yep. The main goal is to get your tower thirteen floors tall and each stack of your cards is a level of the tower," Corbé explained.

"And what are those black cards for?" Lancelot asked.

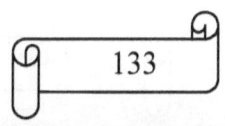

"They start and end the game," Corbé said, placing one on Lancelot's side and one on her side. "The first card is the base and the game ends when one of us gets to the thirteenth floor and places their roof card on their stack."

"Interesting," Lancelot looked to the other piles Corbé was forming. "So, the red, green, and yellow ones are different I'm assuming."

"Reds are residents, greens are artefacts, and yellows are rooms, and all three are required to make a single level," Corbé said.

"I'll learn as we go," Lancelot collected his cards and erected his posture as Corbé took her first turn.

As they played into the deepest hours of the night and early hours of the day, the two of them enjoyed their light conversation and friendly competition.

Mickey Vague was sat on a ring of Saturn, reclining himself onto the plush gas planet and kicking his stubby feet up onto Jupiter. Streaking comets and streams of stardust passed and swirled around the sketchy merchant as he lounged on the planetary furniture. In his paw, the panda fidgeted with Pluto as if it was a large stress ball.

At his distance, he kept his dead eyes on the celestial object three planets away, Earth, the world that was the biggest mystery to him. It wasn't the planet that was bathed in ice, the one that was once infested with speedsters, or the only one that never once housed a form of life. It was Earth. That blue and green orb.

The panda chucked the puny orb he held over his shoulder, it being attracted back into its normal orbital path like it was magnetized to it. He stood and fell forward, laying himself over Mars and Jupiter so he could look at the Earth more closely. He couldn't make out buildings, nor people, nor animals, nor magical features. It merely was just Earth to him.

From the void of space, Mickey plucked his hiking pack from the zero gravity it floated in to retrieve a nutcracker. He placed the moist globe into the nutcracker's jaws and gave it a strong squeeze, but it refused to break against the near infinite amount of force he exerted. With a groan, Mickey discarded the nutcracker into space.

With a pass of his massive paw, the outer Terrace shell of the Earth turned invisible so the inner Dolorous Realm was now revealed. The tint of the yellow sun, Sol, disappeared entirely to only have red be the colour that illuminated the solar system like it was molten steel in a dark forge. Dolorous, which was once a heap of grey rock that only

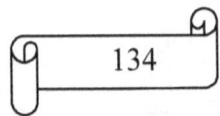

slightly glowed scarlet, was now burning brightly and was covered in vegetation and thriving.

A quick flick of Mickey's wrist spun the colours of Earth through the hues of the rainbow before flashing white and resetting back to the default yellow.

The panda reached over to his hiking pack again to take in a long puff of his hookah. With his exhale, his mind returned to his 'body' that was sat in a primitive observatory of stone and steel. Both the herb and coal had burned away on the panda's hookah, leaving him in the harsh reality of nothing but an empty village of huts, firepits, and dozens of pelts decorating the floor of the observatory.

"Someday soon," The merchant spoke softly, packing his hookah in his hiking to leave the village. "Corbé will realise what a big mistake she's made."

Valentin polished his flute as he laid on his behemoth tongue bed in his pitch black Shroudolous flesh brick room, lightly humming to Colby who had snuggled up against his friend's neck. Only once the Fiend was positive that the rodent was fast asleep did Valentin cease his humming. Inspecting the fife and thinking about his Dolorean escapades, a large portion of his spirit felt like destroying the item would be the best course of action. Valentin's abilities were already quite powerful, but with the flute they were amplified tenfold. By looking upon his wrist at the friendship bracelet that sported his princess friend's name, the conflict in his mind became even more intense.

Before he could make a decision, the Priestess of Shroudolous exploded into the room. Valentin was about to play his flute, but his urgency was misplaced.

"Ah, Valentin," Valaeria released a sigh of relief, placing a hand on her chest. "I labelled you as missing on my census. I thought you'd gone off somewhere."

"Nein, nein," Valentin resettled into his bed. "I've been here."

Valaeria's eyes darted to the golden flute in the Fiend's hand.

"Where did you get that?" She asked.

"This? I've always had it," Valentin said matter-of-factly.

"Not that I recall… And what's that little vermin doing in-?"

Valaeria's sentence was halted by Valentin's melodious tune. Once the song was over, Valaeria shook herself out of her trance.

"Ah, Valentin," Valaeria breathed easily. "I thought you were missing. Guten tag, Colby," The Priestess put on a cute voice to greet the sleeping rat. "Sorry to disturb you two, I'll let you two rest up."

As she left, Valentin allowed himself to relax.

"Woof," Valentin dabbed his forehead of forming sweat. "That decides it, I'm keeping this thing."

The Storey Continues:
The Queen of Dolorous – The Sage of Morholt
Steel thine nerves for:
01110100 01101000 01100101 00100000 01110011 01100101 01100011
01101111 01101110 01100100 00100000 01100100 01101001 01101101
01100101 01101110 01110011 01101001 01101111 01101110